GIL HOGG

DON'T CRY FOR THE BRAVE

Matador
9 Priory Business Park
Kibworth Beauchamp
Leicestershire LE8 0RX, UK
Tel: (+44) 116 279 2299
Fax: (+44) 116 279 2277
Email: books@troubador.co.uk
Web: www.troubador.co.uk/matador

ISBN 978 1783064 670

British Library Cataloguing in Publication Data.
A catalogue record for this book is available from the British Library.

Typeset in 12pt Bembo by Troubador Publishing Ltd, Leicester, UK

Matador is an imprint of Troubador Publishing Ltd

Printed and bound in the UK by TJ International, Padstow, Cornwall

1

I was flown from Hoi An to Saigon for the court martial in a Lockheed C-130 Hercules jammed with military supplies, tired, sleepless, my head full of sparks. The journey to gaol was completed by military police Jeep. I had a minder with me, a military police sergeant, but at this time I was only nominally in custody.

As the Jeep jolted through the outskirts of the city, I could see legions of shabby terraced houses with orange tiled roofs and barred windows, rows of shuttered shops and the wood and tar-paper hovels of the very poor. The driver of the Jeep avoided main roads, choosing narrow streets, lurching over cobblestones worn by the traffic of decades. Open drains full of still water mirrored the low pearl sky; the air smelt of sewage and the fetid sweat of hidden human life. Red good luck papers fluttered over a few ill-fitting doors.

It was a humid mid-afternoon in July and few civilians were about: a bare-footed labourer pushing a bicycle with a sack of vegetables on the handlebars, some black-clad women in straw hats with loaded carrying poles across their shoulders.

I saw a patrol of troops of the Army of the Republic of South Vietnam. Occasionally, armoured cars crept over the intersections leaving swirling bushes of blue smoke.

ARVN sentries with sandbagged defences were stationed at intervals on the sidewalks. I had a sudden glimpse from the Jeep up one side street: a teeming food market beneath a tattered grey canvas. The pulse of the city was still beating.

I was driven to a spacious suburb where the South Vietnamese forces and their allies had occupied a large number of elegant Franco-Vietnamese houses with high sea-wave gables and tall, shuttered windows. The houses were painted in fading primrose and terracotta, the homes of the comfortable classes before Dien Bien Phu.

The perimeter of the area was cordoned with barbed wire, patrolled and guarded like an army camp; but once inside it was an enclave of old colonial mansions, lavishly set in their own lawns and gardens with fountains and pools. The gardens were overgrown, the fountains dead and the pools drained, leaving puddles full of fallen leaves, paper cartons, plastic bags and old newspapers.

The Jeep halted outside one of the mansions. I climbed out, hefted my kitbag and the MP sergeant marched me to the office of the US Commandant of the area. The Duty Sergeant riffled through his in-tray and identified me like a postal package without seeming to look at me.

"Lootenant Robert McDade," he pronounced, his head down, concentrating on the papers. He spoke in a tired monotone. "You are to remain in your quarters unless under escort. Any unauthorised journey will make you a fugitive. Clear, mister?"

I was to be housed in one of the outbuildings, small windowed, low and of heavy stone construction, with peeling whitewash, formerly a store or stable for one of the mansions. I had a sudden gripe at being held in a cell, but I found to my surprise that the interior had been rebuilt to provide self-contained sleeping quarters, a bed-sitting room, a shower room and a kitchen alcove. The small windows kept out the harsh light. The place was not only adequate, it was clean and even luxurious compared to the billets I had become used to in C Company of the 33rd Regiment, 21st Infantry Division.

And there was a walled area outside with a view of the rear of the surrounding buildings.

On the evening of my arrival and all the next day I was left alone. A mute Vietnamese orderly brought a tray of food at mealtimes. I didn't feel like eating or reading, although I had brought a few books. I was too exhausted to do any exercises. Instead, I walked up and down in the yard, eight paces long and half as wide, between showers of rain, until the weeds soaked my boots. I stripped off and lay on the bed, sweating and smoking, wishing childishly that I could shrink to nothing, be forgotten.

I drew from an envelope the letter which had arrived by US Forces special delivery, uncensored, just before I left Hoi An, addressed from the 7th Army General Medical Centre, Saigon.

Dearest, what has happened? I had a note from Jim saying you were in trouble. He says it is pathetic and trivial, but he seemed to think you might be court martialled. He doesn't explain. He says he was in action with you recently and that you were very brave. I'm proud of you for that. But it scares me. Things are awful here, as usual. I'm missing you terribly. Let me hear from you soon. All my love, Gail.

I had to reply. I propped myself up against the head of the bed with a ball-point pen poised over the pad of notepaper I found by the bed. One event had followed another in an unplanned, unexpected way. Starting with the underground tunnel at Kam Sung and the woman who complained about an unjust war... My motives had been a little confused. I hadn't acted at times when I should have, that was sure. But I hadn't actually *done* anything. I hadn't courted trouble or disruption. Events had swept me along. When I had raised my arm it was only a reaction, never a planned and intended motion. It all seemed random and accidental and therefore impossible to explain to Gail in a way in which one event followed another logically…

I crumpled the blank writing paper and sagged into sleep. I dreamed I was in Saratoga Springs in the lounge of Gail's parents' lavish home, in my filthy flak jacket with my boots oozing mud, trying to explain myself to Gail's father. I wasn't sure what I wanted to say. Mr Blake was becoming more suspicious and inaccessible as I hesitated. I awoke, eyes burning, head drumming. I had never met Gail's father or been inside their family home.

I watched and listened to the Vietnamese clerks who occupied the ground floor rear of the mansion over the wall. They worked with the shutters and windows wide open. The clerks seemed sleepy and not too busy; they sometimes joked loudly, chittering like birds in an aviary, and then fell silent quickly as though somebody of importance might overhear them.

The sound of artillery and the crackle of jets were intermittent, the whoom-boom-brrrrr of the 150mm guns like a distant storm. Periods of silence followed when I could hear the moisture dripping from the trees on the other side of the wall, and the quiet chuckling of the clerks. The complex of buildings in my sight was the rear of the Commandant's headquarters. Once, when I was outside, I saw a senior officer walking on the second-floor terrace above the clerks' room, in conversation with a Vietnamese officer. The senior officer saw me watching and moved away from the rail, out of the line of sight.

I listened and waited.

On the second evening after eating I was dozing on the bed. The door was simultaneously rapped and thrown open. A tall staff sergeant stepped into the room without invitation, a reminder that I was in custody. He gave a derisory salute, hardly raising his fingers above chin level.

"Mr McDade? Staff Rostock, sir. Making arrangements for the court."

I looked up at a shaven head and a face wrinkled like a tobacco leaf. I eased up from the bed, naked except for a pair of boxer shorts and slipped into the towel robe which came with the quarters. Staff Rostock held out a piece of paper with four names on it.

"Choose your defending officer, sir. Unless you want to nominate somebody yourself."

I read the names. "I don't know anybody to appoint. I don't really want a defending officer."

"Court will insist. Your interests. Want me to tell you anything about them, the names?"

"Never heard of any of them. I'll take the first one if I have to."

"Amherst? He's OK. They're all OK. Rest are older. Fraser the best. Lot of wins in Guam and Hawaii. Talks like an old uncle."

"Does it matter who does the job?"

"Nah. Judge Advocate General's Corps, sir. All been to college."

"Any more about Amherst?"

"Very quiet man. Take Fraser, sir. He'll keep everybody sweet."

"I'll stick with Amherst."

Staff Rostock's jaw jerked a fraction as though he'd been rebuked. "I'll tell Mr Amherst, sir. He'll get back to you," he snapped, turning on his heel. He marched out, banging the door behind him.

My flash of perversity had made me disregard good advice. Rostock, a twenty year man for sure, would know best. For a moment, I considered calling Rostock back and then hesitated; that would have exposed me, again, to the staff sergeant's contempt.

The next morning at ten o'clock, Amherst arrived at the quarters. His washed-out summer drill uniform bore what appeared to be the newly acquired insignia of a major. He entered the room slightly stooped, his figure bulky around the middle, a large head and small, ineffectual-looking hands. He passed one hand over his thin, dry hair self-consciously and averted his glance, seeming to look curiously at me out of the corners of his eyes. "Geoffrey Amherst."

We shook hands. I pointed to the chair by the bed. Amherst took the chair. I sat on the end of the bed. In the first few moments we scarcely spoke, but instinctively shuffled while we looked each other over.

"Rostock spares no feelings, so I know you chose me off the top of the list," Amherst said.

"So what?"

"The Army is rigidly alphabetical so I usually score where there's a list."

"Is that demeaning?"

"No, but it's common. People do it out of ignorance, or desperation, or bravado."

"I plead guilty to all three. And ignoring advice."

"Ah, Rostock advises on choice does he? Fraser, yes? Well, Fraser's good."

"I'm happy," I said indifferently. I was in shit, and a little deeper didn't seem to matter.

"So am I," Amherst said cheerfully. "This top of the list thing gives me a day in court, and gets me away from the desk work, the divorces, custody fights, debt foreclosures, and all the not-very-absorbing problems of our service people. After all, I joined to get trial experience. My contribution to the war."

I raised my eyebrows. Perhaps I shouldn't have been so indifferent. Was this guy learning on the job? "I hope you've had plenty of experience."

"Enough," he said confidently.

I liked it that at least Amherst wasn't talking himself up as Clarence Darrow II. I guessed he wasn't much older than me. He didn't have any of the marks of combat on him. Lucky man. I did have those marks. My wiry brown hair showed traces of premature grey. My expression was gaunt now; the forehead high, the face long and lined. I used to be six feet tall and a comfortable two hundred pounds; now I looked tall and bony. My teeth and fingers were stained by tobacco like a man careless of his appearance, which I had become. I had a frequent cough, a dry bark; my eyelids were red and weighty, and my complexion had the flush of a heavy drinker. I was a heavy drinker. I hardly recognised this man when I saw him in the mirror. Gail said that I had a 'slightly frayed' charm, which is kindly. Attractive to women? I'd stopped having those thoughts.

Amherst produced a whiskey bottle, Jack Daniels. The gesture gave me a tingle of pleasure. I found two glasses in the kitchen, a bottle of cold, still water from the refrigerator and a six-pack of Pabst Blue Ribbon. Amherst ignored the beer and took the liquor neat, swishing it around in the bottom of his glass and watching the amber tide as we began to talk tentatively, feeling each other out about the progress of the war.

"Giap's Tet offensive, what do you think?" Amherst asked.

"A failure. Yeah?"

"Yep. The US Embassy still inviolate... if a little scarred," Amherst added.

We exchanged calculating looks, each man trying to determine how well grounded the other was, and where he stood politically.

7

"Khe Sanh held," Amherst asserted.

"With six thousand marines. Hell, six thousand!"

"We'll win," Amherst said, wearily.

"At a cost," I admitted. "Roll on 1969 and the day of victory!"

"No way the most powerful nation on earth can be defeated by… " Amherst began heavily.

"By who, Geoff? Who are we fighting? North Vietnam? Communism? Hundreds of thousands of Charlies? Giap? I don't know."

"I guess… we're fighting a little-known eastern general in essence," Amherst said lightly.

A series of head movements and grunts and mm-mm sounds brought us to a shared conclusion without enthusiasm or patriotism, a depressing assessment of what we both thought of as the inevitable victory, but pyrrhic or not, a victory.

Amherst changed the subject abruptly. He extracted a file from his leather case and balanced it on his knee. "I haven't studied the case papers, Bob, just skimmed them. You're supposed to have refused a command and assaulted your CO."

"Sure. That's what happened," I said candidly, exhaling a funnel of smoke from my cigarette.

"I wouldn't give up yet. They're not hanging offences."

"Nothing can change what happened." I picked threads of tobacco from my lips.

"No need to. We'll add a few comments. It's all a matter of how it looks on your day in court. Presentation is everything."

I swung my head up and focused on the lawyer's objective, slate-coloured eyes. "I don't want to go into why this and that happened. Nobody really knows."

"Right, Bob, dead right. Nobody really knows. That's why we have to tell it our way."

"I don't want to tell it my way or any other way."

"You have no alternative. Tell your story or listen to the prosecutor putting across *his* story. You'll mess your pants listening to it. That's why you have to speak up. You know why you did it?"

I gave a spurt of nervous laughter and moved my head, after a pause, in an uncertain 'no'. "It all kinda happened around me. Like I was a dummy."

"Are you sick?"

I made another uncertain negative head movement. "No sicker than anybody else around here."

"Yeah, we're all crackers, but you remember what happened? All of it?"

"Most."

"You have blackouts, headaches?"

"Headaches. Doesn't everybody?"

"You'll have to be examined by a medical board."

"OK. I want to plead guilty. Get it over."

"What about the consequences?" Amherst had a lopsided grimace which signified that it wasn't very funny. "Discharge in disgrace. Or reduced to the ranks. Detention. The word'll follow you into the high street."

I was silent. This was something I'd never considered in my impetuous behaviour. The thought of being sent home in disgrace, being identified in the town as a veteran who couldn't cut it. However tough the battle, however unreasonable the stress, there was an unwritten and unspoken rule that the troops carried the burden, dying of injuries, maimed, going mad, but they didn't quit. No quitting. OK, a few shat themselves and ran away, but relatively very few. And that unwritten and unspoken rule was accepted as gospel in every town in every state at home.

I helped myself to another gulp of whiskey to allow thinking time.

"Maybe you don't care about the consequences." Amherst spoke dispassionately, and watched me carefully.

"I care, but I haven't much confidence in a stage-managed defence." I thought of a film with Amherst as director, the kind of slick trial presentation you see in the movies.

Amherst's lips twisted like a father dealing with an obtuse child. "Bob, all defences are stage-managed. On the question of your confidence in *me*, I don't mind whether you have it or not. You're not paying me. But you better understand the process you are going to suffer or you'll be minced up like sausage meat. And when you understand the process, your basic intelligence will tell you, you *have* to respond."

"Jawing about this in court is going to make it worse."

"Listen, you're the turkey, I'm the cook."

"I thought I was going to be a sausage?"

"Good," Amherst smiled. "A lot of small things go in your favour. The Court will be reluctant to convict an officer. If they can decently let you off, they will. They're not a hanging jury out to get you. All they need is a plausible reason… "

"Refusing to obey your CO when Charlie's outside the wire is difficult to put plausibly."

"Leave that to me. The Army doesn't want this trial. We're supposed to be fighting a war, not playing judges and lawyers. You'll get the benefit of haste. They won't take much convincing that what happened to you should have been handled by your CO as a little domestic problem. They won't thank him for pushing his problems upward."

"You make it sound easy."

"No. The charges are serious. Very serious. But on what I know at the moment the facts aren't. We may be able to make the charges look like technicalities, but it won't be easy. I'll need to know everything you know about what happened. And I mean everything."

I had a fair idea of what Amherst was thinking: how to control the emotions and prejudices which can blow like storm winds around a case; uncertainty whether I was ill, or a hardhead, or a coward playing to be sent home, or possibly a good guy in a bad scene, now wanting, for shame, to get it behind him as quickly as possible. I was too confused to work out which of these assessments was the real me.

"No harm in telling you about it," I said.

Amherst passed the bottle. "Where y' from?"

"Son of a trucker, born Rochester, New York State twenty-five years ago. Grew up and schooled in Saratoga Springs. Graduated from Rochester City College, a major in English and history, thinking of teaching. Volunteered to get an edge rather than be drafted. At City we didn't understand what was happening. We had ROTC guys beating war drums and peaceniks painting *Fuck Johnson* on the walls of the campus dorms. I wouldn't have recognised the chicken track sign if it had been tattooed on my ass."

Amherst agreed. "Same here. No perspective. How can you get perspective at college when you're thinking of baseball and screwing?"

"How did *you* get here?" I asked the question because I still wasn't confident about this guy in whose hands my future might rest. Although I was too confused to work out my own direction of travel from here, I was worried about having my fate complicated by an incompetent.

"My folks are hardworking farmers in North Dakota, and my mom indoctrinated me from an early age that I had to be a doctor or a lawyer, and in default *anything* but a farmer. Some smartass law grads were working on ways to dodge the draft, but my folks expected me to serve. Joined the Judge Advocate General's Corps, figuring I'd get trial experience and stay out of the firing line." He made a nervous sweep with his hand over his scalp.

"The soft option."

"Frankly, yeah."

I liked him for admitting it. With hindsight, I'd have taken the soft option too if there'd been one. "Where are you going to bestow your trial experience when we win this war?"

"I fancy a small-town general practice in the Mid-West somewhere. Court work yes, but a mixed bag: property, probate. Comfortable and quiet. You?"

"As I said, teaching, but who knows, now? Been in 'Nam two years. Second tour. Firefights on long-range patrols. Several offensives. A bit of shrapnel scratched my butt but otherwise nothing."

"You've been lucky." Amherst nodded respectfully. He could see what I already recognised: the span from ROTC rookie, athletic and decisive, to the vet, hesitant, vacillating, clouded by depression. "It takes a toll."

"Do you think the prosecutor might think I'm looking for a way out of the Army?"

"Are you?"

"I don't think so. Not even subconsciously. I'm like everybody else, I guess. This is one fuck-up of a war, but I have to play a reluctant part until we get it done."

Amherst considered. "I don't know. The prosecutor might suggest you're a devious man looking for a way out. It's happening every day."

"Who is he, the prosecutor?"

"Max Vale. Lieutenant Colonel Max Vale. Courts are often swayed by impressions as much as facts, but Max is a man for facts, for detail, not exactly a pedant... but nearly."

"What's he like?"

Amherst shook his head in a private reverie, apparently

reserved in what he could say to a client about his professional brother. "He grinds cases up small."

"Sausage meat?"

"Max is a career Army man."

I was now stretched out on the bed in a T-shirt and shorts, hands clasped behind my head, a cigarette jammed between my teeth. A blue tendril of smoke cottoned up to the ceiling. "You scared of him?"

"Hell, no. He's a goddamned nuisance. He won't let you go easily, that's all. That's why he's a good prosecutor."

Amherst took a legal notepad and pencil from his briefcase and sat back in the easy chair, his pencil poised, his head slightly askew like a conductor waiting to hear the first note from the orchestra.

"Where to start?" I asked.

"Wherever you want. In Saratoga Springs if you like."

"Maybe the starting point is the Springs because that's where I went to school, and Gail was there, but we were never friends. And I observed her brother Jim Blake in the distance. Gail's my fiancée. She's a nurse right here, now, in 'Gon. Jim is a company commander in my unit. Jim and Gail are close. He's Westpoint. A career man. One of the very brightest track athletes and students at Saratoga High in my day. I'm not in the same league as Jim. As I say, we weren't buddies. He was a star. I was a distant admirer. I asked to join this unit because I knew one or two *other* guys from the Springs who were serving. I figured you might as well fight alongside those you know, but actually you don't get to be beside them. I didn't realise, at that time, that I'd become involved with Gail, or meet Jim Blake so close and personal. So there's a starting point... "

13

2

The officers were three or four deep around the bar of the US Forces Officers' Club in Le Loi Boulevard every night to take on fuel for their journey into the small hours. The bar room was chilled by air conditioners, decorated in black and chrome, thick with cigarette and joint smoke, and deafeningly noisy; the noise of urgent, even frantic voices, which at times masked the canned jazz music.

I was newly arrived – three months – and temporarily assigned. I had a shot of rye in my hand and guys from 21st Division HQ, where I was pushing paper, around me. Life in 'Gon was bearable; days spent in cool rooms and clean clothes, poring over plans and reports. Off duty I didn't think too much about the war. I endured the poignancy of Christmas 1966 in a sultry city, hazed with vehicle fumes, its streets occupied by tanks like malevolent beetles. There were bars and women and drugs and enough leisure at night to take advantage of them. I partied desperately in my weeks with the 21st as the date of my posting to C Company of the 33rd Regiment came closer. For a time, there was a possibility that I would be appointed to a desk job in Hoi An as an intelligence officer; but no, for once the Army was going to give a serviceman what he had perhaps foolishly asked for: a frontline regiment.

I was looking across the circular bar which centred the room, at one of the relatively few women officers. I thought she was striking in a pallid way; auburn hair almost shoulder length, a wide brow, glowing eyes. As I went on drinking with my buddies, occasionally joining in the aimless talk, my mind worked on the picture of the girl who was a Nursing Corps captain. I placed myself on the far side of my group to remain sociable but get a clear view through the talking heads. I was almost certain that she was Gail Blake from Saratoga High.

I had never dated her, never danced with her, never been to a party where she was, and as far as I could remember, only taken a few classes which she shared. I couldn't recall any precise meeting or conversation, but I had probably said some inconsequential words to her at classes. But I *had* noticed her at school, learned her name and connected her with her brother, Jim Blake, a sure Phi Beta Kappa three years ahead of us.

And I *had* thought about her at school, as guys do about girls, not in her case about possessing her body, but about her being the kind of girl I'd like to date, without ever seriously considering it could become a reality. She was slim and unsexy then, with angelic looks, a wise, oval face and purplish eyes. My daydreams were more about winning a track event or scoring a home run in her presence, not that I was ever remotely likely to do these things in reality.

In other respects too, the Gail Blake I experienced had been part of a different life. My old man had been a trucker hauling transcontinental rigs who had never been to high school. We were a family of four with my kid brother, our income limited by my father's chronically painful back. There were no books in our home and not much understanding of the value of an education. We had a small house in the Overton area where the men who built the town years ago used to live in cabins. It took Saratoga High to lift my sights to a different kind of life, that which a girl like Gail Blake accepted as normal.

The Blakes, the little I knew of them – learned from talk at school – weren't big-shots; they were the kind of family whose parents were in insurance or accountancy or something else you did with your head, a family that expected their children to go to college and perhaps into a profession.

The truth was that as a kid I was a little embarrassed by the home I came from. I used to imagine what it would be like to have a father who wore a suit and worked in an office; and what it would be like to live in an attractive house, because your house defined you in the eyes of your peers; that was where you *came* from. Often when I was walking the streets of the Springs I'd choose a house I'd like to say was my home; not a palace, a family place with a dash of class: shutters, wide verandahs, a garden with flowers, shrubs and a pond, and in a quiet well-trimmed street. I could anticipate the kind of confidence I would have had if the house I chose was really my home, without, at that early stage, appreciating that what was important was what went on inside the walls.

In reality, our home, on Oak Street, where there were ironically no trees or hedges let alone oaks, was on a small lot of weedy grass close to the sidewalk with a chicken wire fence; it was in a row of similar houses, and faced a similar row across a busy street. Oak Street was a southern through-way for cars and trucks coming to town, and there was always the vibration of vehicle traffic. In contrast, the Blakes lived in the quiet Medina suburbs where the land rolled, and there were streams and trees. The architect-designed houses there exuded a sense of space and calm, or were snuggled away up secluded drives.

The difference in houses said it all. At high school, I couldn't have imagined taking Gail home to meet my mother and have a Coke, any more than I could have imagined being introduced to Mrs Blake in her living room. It wasn't possible and I had lost no sleep in thinking it might be. I had understood and accepted in those days that I was part of one scene and Gail and her kind, another.

But time had moved on. The days were ticking by towards my appointment with sandbags and trenches and jungle slime. I had come to think of my perception of my inferiority as childish and unreal. I was a graduate myself now with career options. I had also realised that the support I'd had from my parents and their peaceful life together had allowed me to live in a warm emotional environment, never mind the clapboard and tiles; it was an environment which I found wasn't as common as I had thought.

I didn't debate with myself whether to make myself known to Gail Blake, who was surrounded by men; I finished my third or fourth shot of rye, thinking the light might go out for me in a matter of months, so what if she did tell me to get lost? What if she said she couldn't remember who I was? What if she wasn't even Gail Blake?

I didn't tell my drinking buddies what I had in mind, I just did it, like in Zen. I circled the bar, pushed into her admirers, eased them out of the way to get to her, received annoyed looks and finally stood before her. She lifted those startling purple-blue eyes to me and smiled with what seemed to be real pleasure and recognition.

"Bob McDade, Saratoga High," I said.

"I know, Bob. I saw you before. I was going to come over." She leaned close to me and put a hand on my arm.

She was going to come over to me? My mouth was dry. I felt knuckles pressing against my spine, and low, disagreeable sounds coming from the officers I had interrupted.

"Who are you, buddy?" one breathed.

Gail frowned. "Come on, guys, lighten up. This is an old friend I have to talk to."

An old *friend*? That was pushing it. She took my hand and eased out of the group. We found a space standing in a corner and began a halting, telegraphic conversation in the noise; where I was posted, where she was posted, what work we were doing; we mentioned scattered reminders of the Springs.

"Let me get you a drink," I said, eventually.

"No, Bob. Don't leave me alone or we'll get separated and you'll have to haul me out – again."

I hadn't hauled her out; that was the remarkable thing. She'd jumped out. I looked around the club distastefully. The vultures were waiting to fall on her. A good-looking and beribboned captain approached her.

"I'll talk to you later, Bill," she said.

The captain moved off, whispering over my shoulder, "May a VC round in excess of 45 calibre find its way up your anal passage, friend."

"What did he say?" Gail asked.

"That I'm one lucky guy."

"Let's go out somewhere, Bob, where we can talk."

I was astonished at the treatment I was getting. "We'll find somewhere to eat."

"Oh, yes!" she said, enthusiastically.

When we left the club together a warm blanket of air enfolded us on the street. The enticing lights of shops and restaurants were juxtaposed with the sinister silhouettes of armed soldiers and military vehicles. Gail pushed her arm under mine and hung on affectionately as though she really was an old friend.

3

I was still puzzled by the reception I had received from Gail at the Officers' Club when we took our seats in Vu Pham's Restaurant on Pleiku Boulevard. I had brought her to Vu Pham's because I wanted a place which was likely to be out of the way of any friends of hers, and yet comfortable enough to give me the opportunity to talk intimately and find some answers.

Vu Pham's had white linen tablecloths, candles on the tables, and excellent seafood. None of the stringency of war showed. About half the many patrons – it was crowded – were in service uniforms, and of those, not all were Americans.

Gail and I drew ourselves into the relative intimacy of a booth and faced each other over tall, cold beers. Gail glanced at the menu and said she couldn't think. "I'll have the same as you, Bob." I ordered peeled king prawns in a chilli sauce from memory. Our seats gave us space; we slipped off our jackets and loosened our ties. I offered her a cigarette and she said she didn't smoke. How little I knew her and how little we had spoken since I shoved into that circle of men around her!

"Hey, this is a nice place," she said, looking round appreciatively but only being polite.

She was tense with phrases and ideas that didn't seem to want to come out. I had a chance to study her. She was more robust now than she had been at school; her face and her figure fuller. The seraphic look remained. Her hair flamed where the light touched it and her smile radiated innocent pleasure. Hers wasn't a sensual face but a wise, touching one that stayed in the mind.

"I felt you were kinda a million miles away when I saw you in the bar tonight, Gail. Mind you, you were about that distance at the High."

"I liked you in Saratoga, Bob. I thought we might be friends at school but it didn't happen."

"That beats me: that you wanted to be friends. I never had a clue."

"Guess I'm not enough of a vamp."

I wasn't going to go into how unattainable I thought she had been; it was part of a past almost too distant to be real. "Anyway, you have plenty of friends here."

"Big deal. Horny guys falling over themselves."

"Uh-huh." I was uncertain what to say because I was surely horny too.

She looked straight at me and reached out her hand to cover mine on the table. "You can be horny too," she grinned.

But I saw the shine of tears in the corners of her eyes.

"It's good to see a face I know, Bob, somebody from home. When I saw you tonight in the club it took me back. I knew I had to speak to you and I was going to come over. I was thinking what to do when I was with those guys. I was worried you mightn't remember me. But I was determined to speak to you. And then you came over to me! I just felt so good and so lucky."

"You OK?" I reached over and put my other hand on her shoulder.

The touching seemed comforting and natural to us both.

"No, I'm not OK. I'm lonely and I'm scared, Bob."

"Lonely I understand. Like in a crowd on the subway. But scared?"

The tears flowed. She picked up the table napkin and sniffed into it, ignoring the food the waiter had placed silently before us.

"Lucky we're in a decent restaurant, I mean one with real linen," she said, looking at the soiled napkin, her eyes sparkling with the tears.

"Scared, Gail?"

"Scared for you, for all those boys at the club, well maybe not all of them. Some are never going to smell gun smoke except on the practice range."

"Sure." My own subterranean fears stirred.

"I see it every day in theatre, Bob, and I work in a well-equipped hospital, not a field hospital, not a MASH unit. It's murder and mayhem, senseless madness."

I nodded assent, picked up my beer and drained what was left, feeling the sweat break out under my arms. She hadn't touched her beer, or the food.

"Do you want to go, Gail?"

"Yes... I'm sorry, because this is really lovely and I'd like to come here again sometime, with you, but I'd like to go now... "

"Back to quarters?"

"No. I'd like to talk... if you don't mind."

"Sure," I said, wondering what that meant precisely, because talking in the night streets of Saigon wasn't something you could do with any ease.

I looked at the tab and threw some bills on the table, only slightly regretful about the prawns, which looked appetising against the white rice and salad, but I had no feeling that I was being messed about by a trivial woman. I thought that Gail was wound up nearly to breaking point. Chance had put me in the right place at the right time.

When we were out in the hot darkness of the street I

turned her towards me, regardless of the touts and pimps who lurked in the dark, watching. I buried my face in her fragrant neck and she pulled my body toward her tightly, melting into me with soft differences of pressure in different places. I could visualise all her hollows and curves.

"Maybe we can find somewhere to sit," I said, which was wishful thinking.

"There's military police, drunks, beggars everywhere, Bob."

"I have nowhere. My quarters are crawling. The only place I can suggest is we find a small, quiet hotel." I thought there wasn't a chance she would ever agree to this.

She snuggled closer to me and startled me again. "That's it. Take me somewhere where we can be alone."

She was quiet in the dirty Renault cab, with its slashed seats and rattling motor. I gave the address of a clean little hotel on Vo Thi Sau Street where I took local girls occasionally. Gail never said, as a woman might, that I seemed to know the right place.

I had found that in Saigon there was a fringe of mainly Vietnamese women who were not whores but were not integrated with their families; they were shop and bar girls, clerks, telephonists, beauticians, care workers; girls, or more often women in their twenties and thirties, who had little hope of a conventional Vietnamese marriage. They wanted independent lives rather than be buried in spinsterhood within the family home. Many of them probably had the dream of marrying a US serviceman; some really believed they might and a few of them would. It was these women that I had toyed with after I had tasted and been dissatisfied with the mechanical sex of the brothels; they could be pleasant companions in grim times.

Checking in, in the shadowy lobby of the My Tho Hotel,

was accomplished with a few discreet words to the old man behind the desk and the almost invisible passing of greenbacks. We mounted the stairs to the third floor and I shut and locked the door.

"Leave the lights off, Bob."

The room was illuminated by neon lights from across the street which flickered through the tattered net curtain, blue, red and green.

We clung together, standing in the tinted darkness, which smelt of scented disinfectant.

4

As we sat naked on the bed in the My Tho Hotel at dawn
we paid little attention to the need to get a shower and go to
our duties, or to the tiny room we were in, with its stained
wallpaper and bedraggled curtains. We didn't bother to look
through the grimy windowpanes at the crumbling shops and
tenements across the street, or feel the thin, damp towels, or
smell the sickly detergent odour.

I reflected on the speed and unpredictability of the events
of the few hours after our meeting. For me, every feeling was
sharpened; adrenalin was surging under a potential sentence
of what might be maiming or death; for her, the agony of
witnessing agony.

"Hi, pal," I said, placing my arm around her shoulders and
squeezing her gently.

"Me too," she said.

"I mean, really… " My voice croaked.

"I know you do. I'm the same way. I mean it."

Of course she didn't know me any more than I knew her.
My cock surged, but I resisted the impulse to push her back
on the mattress. Gail had moved a part of the past into the
present, a past we shared in a limited way; some common
acquaintances, a few recognised local personalities, walks in
the same parks, watching baseball from the same stands,
shopping in the same stores, seeing movies in the same

theatres, sharing our streets and skies. I was part of her little piece of America, but if you examined our viewpoints more closely I calculated that we might see things from different sides of the street; I wasn't sure about that.

When I thought how this would have played out in Saratoga Springs if there was no war and I met her at this time, I realised that it wouldn't and couldn't. I wasn't a good match for her. We could meet at a class reunion, share a joke about school; we could like the look of each other sexually, but I wouldn't ask her for a date, and she wouldn't expect it. She mightn't think too much of the fact that I was a kid from Overton, but she would know that her father would, and her stepmother and her brother. Her family would be likely to think that Gail deserved a beau with a bit of class; and she, for her part, would have the choice of some attractive and talented men with bucks in the bank. On my side, there would be the almost subconscious impulse that would steer me away into relationships where I felt easier.

Despite the suddenness of our coming together, I sensed that Gail was a discriminating woman and I was flattered by her attention. She was no virgin but the purity of her views, what little I knew of them, seemed to reflect a purity of heart. At first I had thought, absurdly, that she had reached out to me because I really was her secret teenage love; that she had fallen in love with me in high school and been too shy to give any sign. It was a wonderfully romantic illusion which excited me – and took only hours to fade.

What Gail had said very simply when we attempted to dine at Vu Pham's was true. She was loose in a herd of males who wanted to possess her body for sexual reasons alone, and who had neither the time, nor the concentration to deepen the relationship beyond sex. She had spoken of a special friend, a flyer, killed in action more than a year ago. My sudden appearance in the chaos was the incarnation in a person of the home and stability she yearned for, and in her weakness she was clinging to me. And of course, in my weakness, in my increasingly craven fear, I was suddenly clinging to her.

The possibilities and impossibilities didn't grate on me as I considered them. It was 1967. We had met in Saigon. We were immediately and explosively lovers. We would see each other every day we were free as the clock counted down to my departure for Hoi An. We would surf together on a great roller that had to break; it would be ecstasy; it would be pain.

Gail astounded me again before we left the room that morning. "Bob, would you buy me a little ring? Nothing much. I don't want to put you to expense."

She looked at me with completely innocent candour. I saw no trace of guile.

"Protection?"

"Yes."

5

My posting to the 33rd Regiment at Hoi An came through inexorably after Christmas. I was one of four new officers to join at that time; new feet for dead men's boots. I could see my own feelings reflected in the faces of my fellow apprentices as we were unceremoniously dumped by the driver of the truck in front of the Regimental Headquarters at Camp Emerson: studied ease and optimism, but under the skin, fearful apprehension. As new recruits to the front line we had experienced nothing, but we had heard everything and it may have been worse in the telling.

After the introspection of enclosure in the city of Saigon, I was overcome as I looked up at the vast yellow sky, the flimsy buildings of the camp, and the distant hills like sleeping reptiles. One of my companions joked as we jumped from the tray of the truck and hit the red dust, "It's getting closer." And it was; the dragon of war.

We rookies were met by the Adjutant, Peter Weston, clipped in his greetings and trim in his figure. We hoisted our kitbags and followed him to our temporary quarters: two-person cubicles with bunk beds and adjoining showers. Weston allowed us no time. He shepherded us back to HQ to meet the commanding officer, muttering rules and timetables which I hardly heard.

Lieutenant Colonel Vaughan, the CO, was a thin, spider-like man with black hairs on the back of his hands, and a wall eye which meant that you couldn't be sure where he was looking. Vaughan shook hands with each of us and added a personal word of welcome. He got confused between Farnley for A Company, and Freeman for B Company. I was destined for C Company, and to me Vaughan confirmed his study of the paperwork by saying, "You'll find a few buddies from New York State here, Bob."

Later in the mess, Vaughan introduced our company commanders, and the rest of the complement of officers. I didn't recognise the man who lunged out of the crowd around the bar to claim me. He was the track hero and distinguished alumnus of Saratoga High. Jim Blake was intense. He had lost the smooth curves of flesh on his cheeks that I remembered from school, that suggestion of a confident and untroubled upbringing.

I already had a mental picture of Blake from Gail's comments about him. She described him as warm-natured and withdrawn. I already knew he was clever academically and of course a distinguished sportsman. Gail had said that their childhood was tranquil, despite the departure of their mother with another man. She said her brother had scarcely spoken to his mother since then. He was fourteen at the time and he never liked the stepmother he was presented with a few years later. Blake had a lot of girlfriends, but Gail thought she was the woman in his life, which she accepted in a motherly way; they were friends and confidants.

Blake immediately took me aside and said that any person close to Gail was OK with him. Gail had written to him saying she was engaged, a surprising plan assembled by us overnight at the My Tho Hotel and unhesitatingly confirmed in the following weeks, and Blake treated this as though it was entirely natural. I anticipated that he had looked at my personal file, knew who my parents were, where I lived, my graduate qualifications, my ROTC service. There was not much in the record to concern or disappoint, and not much to please if you thought your sister was a princess. Not surprisingly, he had no memory of me from high school, which he frankly admitted.

Blake eyed me critically, but I guessed that I had passed the preliminary inspection. I was uncomfortable at having this special connection with a superior officer. In future I would be under surveillance to a degree.

In appearance Blake was unlike his gentle sister. Perhaps the only physical quality they shared was the blue-purple eye colouring. He was over six feet tall with a powerful physique from his hundred metre days. The strength of his shoulders and triangular back was not obscured by his uniform. He had a square head of short, clipped fair hair, a prominent jaw and deep eye sockets. His expression was good humoured but I had the feeling that this covered the essential hardness one would expect of a seasoned infantry captain.

"Going to get hitched, huh?" Blake said, when the beers and whiskey chasers had been set up on the bar. He spoke in a detached way as though this was a far distant event, which it probably was.

"When I'm out. After VV Day."

"The Springs?"

"Maybe. Gail would like that."

"What'll you do?"

"I'm thinking of teaching."

"Teaching high school?"

There was a touch of incredulity in his voice at first, but I thought that was only the gut reaction of a man who had set his sights very high. It was obvious that the cataclysm we were in was changing the shape of our thinking. The old perspectives, seen from Saratoga Springs, were blurred. All that really mattered was that his sister had a decent, reliable guy.

After dinner a group including Blake played cards, and although I would have liked to go to bed, I felt obliged to make my exit with Blake. We talked of baseball, football, basketball, and the pleasures of Saigon. Not a word about the war. Most of us were drunk.

When the poker game was over, and it was past twelve, Blake rallied the mess to a game of forfeits. If you didn't drink your beer down continuously, you had to replenish everybody else, and finish yours. So the game progressed from person to person to the last man standing. It was the kind of contest I would never have entered willingly, but I felt constrained to follow Blake and he encouraged me.

Weston came into the bar occasionally and watched from the shadows, but made no move to break up the party. Colonel Vaughan had retired long before.

The officers played the game shouting, joking raucously, slopping drink on the floor, and falling over each other, seeing those with weaker heads go down on their knees and crawl away. Blake seemed to be half a foot taller than anybody else, urging us on. I remembered him standing over me triumphantly as I subsided helplessly in a heap under the table and passed out amid guffaws of laughter.

A month after my arrival at Camp Emerson, Gail wrote that she would be visiting the Hoi An field hospital with the Surgeon General's inspection team and we might get a chance to meet briefly. With Peter Weston's help I called the General Military Hospital in Saigon and spoke to Gail.

"I'll be on duty all the time, Bob, but according to the schedule we'll be lunching at the hospital, and one and a half hours has been allocated. I'll see you then."

"I'll sort out my end," I said. I would be working with my platoon and therefore would be my own boss for a few hours.

On the day, I commandeered a Jeep and drove to the hospital. I parked and strolled around the wide verandah of the building. I saw a figure standing by the entrance watching me.

"Got a painful injury, Lieutenant?" Blake said, smiling, but not appearing to be pleased.

"I arranged to meet Gail."

"I thought I'd say hullo to my little sister."

Gail burst out through the doors into the awkward silence. After a few moments of reunion hugs, she said, "What am I going to do with you boys?"

Blake looked at me with stony amusement. "Well, Lieutenant?"

I thought Blake was trying to pull his seniority. "Look," I said, "I'll take off and leave you two. Maybe if I come back around 13.45 I can have a word with you Gail, before you go."

"Good idea," Blake grinned.

"OK, Bob," Gail said, "but please be here at, say, half-one. I have to see you."

"Sure," I said, and walked away smarting. At least Gail had split the time equally.

I drove the Jeep idly around the vast workshop of vehicles, tanks, field guns and prefabricated bridges until the heat was uncomfortable. I stopped at the officers' mess. I had a beer and some idle chatter with other officers, and returned to the hospital on time. Blake and Gail were waiting on the verandah. Blake broke away and marched off without greeting me.

I embraced Gail and we went inside. "What did you two do?" I asked.

"We went into the canteen and had a coffee and a sandwich. I'm sorry, Bob. Jim knew I was coming, but it was you I intended to meet. He just turned up and he isn't used to sharing me."

"OK. That's the way it is. Is there somewhere we can go for half an hour?" I asked, looking through the canteen doors at the crowd.

She squeezed my hands. "I've spoken to the sister-in-charge and I can show you one of the new operating theatres. I know you'll be interested," she said, with the dimples in her cheeks showing.

"Just what I wanted to see."

She led me through doors which she unlocked and re-locked as we walked into an area under refurbishment. In a side room there were gurneys and mattresses, paint pots, brushes and stacks of plasterboard. She pulled a mattress from a pile and spread it on the floor. Our disordered clothing and haste was exciting, and there was a sweetness in her reaching out to me which lingered long after the event.

I had another week training with my platoon before we were in a force which was dumped south of Khe Sanh. The area had been pounded with 150mm shells and partly defoliated; it was raked over by the M60s of the Bell UH1 Huey gunships which transported us. We were part of the line that would advance through several villages in a clearance operation.

I had plenty of military tactics in my head, a knowledge of how to maintain and use our weaponry, mainly M16 rifles, an understanding of our wireless communications and scrambler, and even a smattering of insight into tasks considered of a lesser order, like first aid, trenching and food hygiene; but I had nothing I could call real experience of any of these things.

I knew the names of my men. I had talked a little with

each of them and seen their records, but I had no idea of their capabilities. Three were rookies like me; the remainder, including Sergeant Bertolucci, were battle-hardened. I was received when I first met them, rightly, with joky unease and suspicion. It would take time before I obtained more than nominal obedience from them. In the meantime, I would have to rely on Sergeant Bertolucci. He appeared to me to be a depressive character, but at times when I was with the platoon at ease, usually eating or drinking, he could show that Italian sense of enjoyment of the moment which was infectious.

I managed to survive our first day in action, which included exchanging fire with the Viet Cong, because I was preoccupied with my role. I had to get my platoon forward in company with those platoons on either side, through a defoliated forest. I had to manage the search through two villages, where thankfully we found nobody alive. We, with the rest of the Regiment, theoretically 'cleared' an area of about two miles by three miles before other troops dug in on our line, and we were scuttling through the dust to get aboard the Hueys and back to camp. There was no satisfaction amongst the soldiers in the Huey that a good job had been done; rather there was cynicism that anything useful had been done at all, and a sense of relief that we had all come through it, whole.

This was the first of many advances and patrols which went on for two tours of duty over two years. I endured them, like most of the other soldiers, silently questioning the wisdom behind them but resigning the judgment to those above me. I was scared whenever we were in combat, not so much for my life, as for the integrity of my body; dying wasn't going to be difficult, but living in a wheelchair was. None of this weakness, which equally affected my comrades in arms, subverted our determination to fight when called upon. I fought with desperation and so did my men.

I didn't watch over my men as closely as I should have; of the men in the three different platoons I commanded over the period, one died in a booby-trapped village hut, three in firefights, and a fourth committed suicide. When I saw Pfc Cotton, twenty-two years old, sitting on the muddy floor of the jungle with his lunch ration around him, uneaten, staring into space, I should have realised that he was ill, but my reaction was to kick him into action; and he ended his own life that night with his M16.

I was able to see Gail occasionally when she flew north with an ANC inspection team, and when I was on leave in Saigon or when I could hitch a ride down there. Our relationship was stretched out very thinly in these meetings, and in correspondence, but it was a lifeline for us both. When I say lifeline, I mean it helped me having this woman whose agony about whether I was going to get through my duty and finish whole was as acute as mine. It was in a sense selfish, but her need to have a decent home-town boy while she bloodied her hands in the operating theatre was also selfish. Did I love her? I really never had an opportunity up to this time to get to know her well enough, but I did love everything I knew about her. We were dependent on each other.

6

West Quang Tri Province, June. Dawn. I was seated on my pack, my back resting against a sapling. My poncho was around my neck and enclosing me like a tent. I was unsure whether I had slept at all. A vapour like rotting fish wafted up inside the poncho. I suppressed a painful sense of absurdity. The members of my patrol were around me, wraiths in the foliage. I levered myself stiffly to my feet.

"How long do you reckon, sir?" Sergeant Lucas moaned.

Lucas was asking for the benefit of the men near him. Nothing was as warming as the anticipation of re-entering our lines.

"Four hours, maybe six," I said.

"Make that ten. Or fifteen," Trask said.

I wiped the palm of my hand over my bristling chin and met his impudent eyes. "We'll make it soon enough."

Moore stood over the PRC 77 scrambler. "Waterlogged. Dead."

"If it's dead, bury it," I said.

"Yeah, we'll have a funeral, 'Rest in peace communication with the outside world...'" Schuyler said.

"Shut it," Lucas replied. And to Moore, he said, "You'll be thirty pounds lighter. Take these M70 rounds."

"Hey, Sergeant... "

We eventually started moving, stumbling through slime, fending off the embrace of entwined branches, breathing the hot breath of the rainforest, watching patterns in the trees, straining to hear, massaging the steel of our rifles.

The dawn darkened. Bulging clouds disgorged a torrent. The rain beat on the leaves, an orchestrated roar obliterating other sounds. We groped and choked and splashed forward.

The rain stopped suddenly. In the new silence, above the tapping of the dripping leaves and the sluicing of water at our feet, another noise: the distant moan of an aircraft.

"Light plane. Spotter," Sergeant Lucas said.

"Whassa time?" somebody asked.

"Seven," Lucas said. "Time for chow, sir?"

"Sure," I said, looking up through the branches at a grey rag of sky. I checked my watch. My white wrist looked vulnerable, like the whiteness of the throats of my troops; we were soft white bugs in shells.

Lucas posted sentries. We slid out of our packs, squatting amongst the vines and fallen trunks, retreating into the rain-dark of our flak jackets and ponchos. Dirty, tense faces slackened as we eased our patrol harnesses, draped with grenades and spare magazines, and settled our M16s near us.

"Beef?" Lucas said, squinting at a packet of C-rations.

"My ass. Dog meat," Schuyler said.

"Keep quiet," I said.

I listened, turning away from them to concentrate. The trees were beginning to thin out; but the infinitely shaded green of the supple trunks around us was still the ever-enfolding bars of a cage. "Hear anything, Sergeant?"

"Nah. I smell bacon and eggs." Lucas was a first generation Greek-American, a man with a lust for food. His full lips curled as he juggled packets of rations.

"Now, your VC is reclining in his black pyjamas eating boiled rice," Trask said.

The men shared out the packets, bantering feebly. I searched their faces unsuccessfully for signs of resolution which would infuse strength into me. I moved away, flakes of biscuit pricking my dry tongue. I gulped warm water from my bottle. Was that gunfire? An aircraft? We had to move. We were blundering forward. I could imagine the phantoms encircling us, almost see the black snouts prying toward us through the undergrowth.

Around my boots was a pool of water; it reflected a creased face with stained eye sockets. The man who had *volunteered* to look into this puddle in this place at this moment. I could be stretching between dry sheets, hearing the milkman rattle the bottles at the gate, flicking on the bedside radio for the news. *US fighter-bombers made ten strikes yesterday at railway yards and ammunition storage areas near Hanoi… Units supporting the US 21st Infantry Division reported no casualties after a light engagement… A patrol on routine reconnaissance duty in the western provinces is overdue and reported missing, bringing the month's total of troops killed or missing to…*

"My wife's birthday today," Moore said, and frowned. "Or was it yesterday?"

"What day is it?" Schuyler asked.

"What does it matter?" Trask said, fingering a small snapshot of the birthday wife in a plastic envelope which Moore had handed around.

"You guys been told Charlie will use the crap in your pockets. You shouldn't have it. Put it away," Lucas said.

"Moore's an optimist. He thinks Charlie won't get us," Trask said.

The words snapped me back to the shrunken limits of our world: the jungle. Existence before, and existence after, increasingly unbelievable.

"Can we verify our exact position, sir?" Lucas asked.

I pretended I was still listening to the sounds around us. The theory of map reading was easy but the practice wasn't.

When you march day and night across a hilly trackless wilderness, where every stream and every hill and every paddy look the same, where rain and mists reduce visibility and your radio fails, you lose your reference points. "I'm going to plot our exact position in a moment," I said calmly.

My bowels wrenched. I sweated and clenched my fists. At any moment a feather of smoke could come from the vines.

"I'll tell you where we are," Trask said. "We're fuckin' well up shit creek without a paddle!"

"Not so much mouth, soldier," Lucas said.

I wiped the mud from my hands on my jacket and unrolled an oilcloth mapcase. The map, a veiny yellow cadaver, I spread on the ground between my knees. I placed my compass on the map and orientated it; blurring spots of water dripped on to the surface.

"Are we here to prove we can survive like swamp birds?" Shuyler asked.

"Can it!" Lucas said.

"We've gathered useful info," I said, keeping my eyes on the map, not wanting to see the rightly incredulous looks on the faces of my men.

"Can you pinpoint where we are, sir?" Lucas pressed.

I observed Lucas as I considered my reply; the pale, oily face under the vizor of his helmet, matted black hair sticking to his forehead, insubordinate eyes weighing the competence of his leader.

"Sure, Sergeant."

The lie itself was easy; a level, faintly irritated voice to rebuke a noncom who should know better. I tapped the map definitively.

The official orders were so damn simple. *Reconnoiter and report on enemy units, and possible observation posts to enable field artillery fire to be directed… Return and report.* By the time

Command HQ had considered our report with all the others, and with aerial photos, what we said would be submerged, confused. Our mistakes wouldn't even be verifiable.

"We proceed here," I said, tracing a river artery south and east. I moved the map so the route was unclear to the watchers. I brought firmness to hollow faces. My leadership, at least at that moment was immutable, a metal albatross locked around my neck. If I failed, we'd all perish. "By tonight you'll be on your bunks having a smoke."

"Oh yeah? Cleaning shithouses… "

"Yeah, any time."

I confidently circled a proposed observation post on the map and pointed to a hill in front of us. "I'm going up to take a look. About an hour. I'll take Moore with me."

Moore ditched grenades, M70 rounds, a Claymore mine, entrenching tool, and one plastic canteen. He settled his M16 at the ready in the crook of his arm. I swung my machete while I waited. Sergeant Lucas moved closer to me, shutting the others out.

"We could get our asses shot off here," he said.

"Get on with it, Sergeant."

"What happens if you're not back in an hour?"

I narrowed my eyes in exasperation. "Call a cab and put it on my expenses."

Moore and I climbed using animal tracks, bending double to get through dense branches. I dodged across the slope seeing easy paths and avoided hacking a noisy trail. The growth began to thin. I moved faster, stopping every few moments to listen. I heard only my pounding arteries and the tack-tack of water dripping on leaves.

We came into a pearly light. A hawk was poised far above us on a stream of air.

I found a knoll and climbed a lone tree which gave me a

limited vision across the hills. With my field glasses focused I couldn't find any feature that I could relate to the map. I slid down to the ground. "We're on the right track. It's cool," I said.

We rejoined the patrol within the hour, and in another hour I had led them over a ridge to a view of a disused plantation. I couldn't place the plantation on my map, but I said I could. I was desperate. I was insanely leading my patrol into the jaws of the enemy! We picked our way goat-like down slippery open slopes, our movement hopefully obscured by clouds of mist and rain. About three hundred feet above the plantation the ground began to fall more gently, and we entered thick trees tangled with vines and undergrowth. We rested.

"That's a hell of a way we've come," Lucas said.

"There's no fuckin' going back," Trask said.

"We'll get closer to the plantation and decide whether we go through or around," I said.

The patrol, with me leading and Lucas at the rear, felt its way downward like a caterpillar seeking the way of least resistance, nerves taut. A lightness overhead, the surprise finger of the sun on my forehead, drew my attention from the descent. Above the head-high bush, I could see two thatched sheds surrounded by a bamboo fence.

I scanned the huts with field glasses. "Deserted."

"There's somebody there," Schuyler said.

Steam quivering in the heat rose from the foliage blurring our vision.

I swung the glasses across the scene again. "Yes, there is somebody."

"Oh shit," Trask said.

A soldier in camouflage kit was standing motionless at the edge of the thicket.

"A guard," I said.

"Trouble," Lucas said.

"We'll watch for a while," I said.

Lucas gave me a reproachful look. We were pinned to the foot of the hillside we had descended. The paralysing question was whether we should flee back up the slope, and possibly be seen.

7

Decide. Go forward. Go around. Do the impossible, go back. A few moments for me to make a decision which would save or kill us. It had to be an arbitrary decision; it was too late for reasons and plans.

"We'll go around."

"Why don't we charge with fixed bayonets?" Schuyler asked.

I turned round to the petrified faces. "We'll go down and round. We can be past in an hour. Another two, and we're behind our lines."

It was the absurd over-simplification which the men all wanted to hear and it served to rouse them. We crept for twenty minutes on all fours. The huts came into view more clearly beyond the trees. We gathered to watch.

"Wait," Sergeant Lucas whispered.

A figure was crossing the yard, walking close to the fence, which was as tall as his head. I pressed my eyes to the field glasses. The furry image of the man jigged up and down. "Steam on the bloody lenses!" I wiped them with my forefinger.

"Let me look, sir," Lucas said, taking the glasses from me.

Lucas fingered the adjustment. "Jesus and Mary!"

I reached for the glasses. Lucas held on.

"That's not Charlie. It's one of ours, by God! Wait. He's talking to the sentry, helmet off, wiping his face. Fair skin and hair. I can see it."

I was able to see enough when I had the glasses back to convince myself it was true. A feeling of silent joy overcame and relaxed us all. We really smiled for the first time that day.

"It's no use trying to attract their attention from here. They'll only start shooting. We need to get within earshot so that they can hear us unmistakably," I said.

A half an hour later the patrol had worked itself into a position on level ground, fifty yards from the huts, which were clearly visible through a thin patch of saplings. I had been speaking in whispers for days. Could my dry throat produce a full voice? I stood up, my men on the ground behind. Light glittered in the leafy void around me. I cupped my hands around my mouth.

Before I could shout, a blast of automatic rifle fire sprayed the trees. I had a sensation of whirling fragments of branches and chips of wood. I flung myself to the ground, breathing the reeking leaves.

I put my head up. "You fucking assholes!" I shouted.

Silence.

"Suppose we were wrong?" Trask said.

"Screw this," Lucas said, up on his knees. "Hey, US Army patrol here you asswipes!" The words came out in a roar from Lucas' corded throat.

The rifle squirted again.

"Damn fools!" he shouted.

We heard a laugh.

"Come out with your hands up," a loud American voice said calmly.

"Do as they say," I said.

We got to our feet and moved silently through the thinning bushes to a clearing in front of the fence, our arms sagging down like broken wings. Through a gap in the fence we faced a trio of armed GIs. The air was bright and unbreathably hot.

"Well, Bob McDade and his posse." Jim Blake sauntered toward me and put an arm round my shoulders. "Great to see you, buddy."

Blake's men were amused.

"Bloody swine!" Lucas declared.

"You look like shit-scared Boy Scouts, lost on a Sunday ramble," Blake said. "Go in the hut and take a break."

I followed Blake to the hut where his men who weren't on lookout rested in the shadows. We stood outside under the wide eaves.

"We've had a bit of luck," Blake said. "Rounded up a bunch of VC and sympathisers. How about you guys?"

"We're heading back. Overdue, but it's been worth it." I tried to sound confident.

"Show," Blake said, pointing at a map which he unrolled.

I slipped my own map out of my pack and spread it out on the ground. My mind stalled. I had nothing to contribute. Blake pointed to the markings on my map and looked into my eyes, shaking his head negatively. We were both conscious that our men were within earshot.

"Yes, I'm sure… " I began trying to think of an excuse for being lost.

"This is where we are." Blake pointed to another quarter of the map. "We'll go together, OK, Bob?"

I was grateful for Blake's gentle, uncritical tone. "Sure," I said. At least I wasn't going to be revealed as incompetent in front of my men.

Blake had always maintained a certain distance in camp as befitted his pedigree and seniority, but he wasn't shy about his special connection with me. There had been occasional brief threesomes with Gail for a meal when she visited our various camps. She wrote frequently to each of us telling me about her brother, and her brother about me. But my view of Blake started to diverge from Gail's portrait from the first night that we met in the mess at Hoi An. Blake had a nickname more applicable to a general than a captain, 'Iron Jim', won from his men for an unyielding attitude to hardship and adversity. He had begun to stand out as a man who had a voracious appetite for war.

"When do you plan to move?" I asked him.

"When we've finished the interrogation. Come and see."

8

I left my men resting and went with Blake to the second hut. The smell of the dark interior as I blinked on the threshold was the butcher-shop odour of blood, and the stink of excrement and half-digested food. An officer knelt on the floor with his back to the door. He looked round as we entered. I recognised him as an interpreter, Captain Nguyen, a South Vietnamese officer attached to C Company.

Two prisoners were roped against the wall; they were crumpled down on their haunches. One was a woman of about thirty in a black shirt and pants with her hair hacked short. The other was a man of about the same age, hollow-chested and sick-looking. As my eyes became accustomed to the gloom I counted eight more people roped together at the far end of the hut, sitting silently, their knees drawn up and their heads downcast. Some of them seemed like children of perhaps twelve or fifteen years.

"We flushed them out of the tunnels at the edge of the clearing," Blake said.

On the other side of the hut was a body, flat on its back with bare ankles and feet. I looked past the wide feet with their broken toenails toward where the head should have been. The bloody stump gleamed in the shadow.

"What happened?" I asked concealing my retch.

"Part of interrogation process," Nguyen said in a high, precise voice.

Blake and I stood mutely regarding the scene for a moment.

"Will we find out anything useful?" I asked.

"Let's see what Nguyen can do," Blake said.

I returned to the rest hut. My men took turns with Blake's in maintaining a ring of lookouts. Even in this hut with the patch of sunlight creeping across the mud floor from the entrance, I felt the foulness of violent death around me like a cloak, and heard the murmured Vietnamese of the interpreter in my ears like tinnitus. The haze of noon hung over the jungle hills. My eyes watered; in the far distance, artillery gunfire and the occasional crackle of warplanes.

I agreed to take a turn on watch with the men. I did so to get away from the rest hut. Here the talk alternated in a quiet hysteria. The men speculated morosely about the risks facing them on the journey back to our lines, and then hilariously about what they were going to do when victory was declared. I couldn't face being with Blake and Nguyen in the slaughter hut either.

I settled myself in a trench beyond the broken bamboo fence. I could see for about three hundred yards through fern and creeper into the darkness of the jungle. Ahead, I had a view across a paddy field which was dry and pocked with shell holes, into the purple brightness. In a way, I deliberately didn't try to work out what was happening around me. I slipped a letter from Gail – which I shouldn't have been carrying – out of my pocket. *7th Army GMC Saigon. My dearest Bob, I think of you all the time and pray for your safety. And I think of you especially when I get into bed at night naked and dream of going to sleep in your arms. And I think and dream of more than just going to sleep. I think of you inside me and your magic fingers on me, and of a big love welling up like a fountain. I can't help writing like this, I love you so. Same as ever at GMC, except I'm doing more admin and less theatre. My rank as captain is substantive now, so attention Lieutenant! All my love, Gail.*

I dozed for a while, horny in the sun. I was hungry. The haze of early afternoon was stifling. I was tired, so tired that the gnawing in my belly could not keep me from longing for sleep between white sheets… but it was a hopeless longing; sleep was a demon that taunted me from afar. Occasionally, in the distance I could hear artillery gunfire and the drone of transport planes. My eyes throbbed trying to detect alien movement where all was quivering and scorching. I had been here for nearly one and a half hours.

Impatient at waiting for food or relief from the duty, I left the thicket and crept towards the huts. Three soldiers were sitting near the door of the rest hut, the remains of a meal scattered round them. I pointed to my mouth and a thumbs-up came from a disembodied arm in the doorway. I'd been understood. I crept back to my post. A few minutes later Schuyler sidled out of the foliage with a tin plate covered by his dirty palm. I took the plate. It was a mess of powdered eggs and pasta, with traces of dust and small leaves in it.

"You dropped it."

"Not actually dropped, sir."

"You know I've been waiting here."

"We thought you were coming over."

Schuyler gave nothing away except a trace of stupid amusement. It was a case of eat this shit or go hungry, soldier.

"Tell Sergeant Lucas to report to me now. That's an order."

"Yes, sir. Mr Blake's making progress with the prisoners."

"What progress?"

"Cutting their throats."

Schuyler sidled away and I swallowed the glutinous mess in four or five lumps.

I had agreed with Blake that we would move at 1300 hours regardless of the success of the interrogation; it was shortly after 1200. I swung my pack on my shoulder and looked at the earth at my feet for signs of my presence. I ground a lump of pasta into the dust, and scanned the jungle and paddy slowly one more time.

Lucas crept to my elbow. "What's going on?" I asked.

He looked hard at me, wrinkled his lips and didn't reply. He cocked his rifle.

"You carry on here," I said.

I approached the big hut along the fence line; there was no shadow. I crept in a shimmering haze. At twenty feet I could see in the doorway the luminous shape of a bare body, the lower back and buttocks of a GI. By the time I was at the door frame, the GI was coming out, tucking his shirt and tightening his belt. Nguyen sat on his haunches outside, under the eaves. Blake was standing beside him, scanning the jungle, his long pale eyelashes nearly resting on his cheeks. The thumb of one of his hands was hooked in his belt; his forearm had fine fair hairs which sparkled.

I stepped past both men into the hut. The woman lay flat on her back on the earth. She stared. Her trousers had been removed and dropped over her thighs. I reached down and pulled the garment away. She whispered some words. I saw the bruises, the blood and wetness between her legs. Nguyen came in.

"What's she saying?"

"Americans would say 'unjust war'."

Her legs were strewn brokenly apart. Her shirt had been pushed up to the rise of her breasts. The contours of her waist and hips shone faintly, smooth and shiny. Below her navel were whitish lines, the stretch marks of an earlier pregnancy. She was probably a mother. I dropped the pants back on top of her body.

"Men need a woman," Nguyen laughed, puffing a cigarette held in a delicate hand. He nodded as though his head was on a rocking pin.

"If she'd had a chance, she'd have cut your balls out," Blake said, entering the doorway as though he could hear my unvoiced objection.

"Did they talk?"

"Sure," Blake said. "It's no time for squeamishness. We may save lives with what we know from this vermin."

"Will we be taking them back?"

Nguyen smiled tolerantly. "Too far."

"This isn't ROTC manoeuvres Bob, hoisting your prisoner's underpants up the flagpole. That stuff."

Blake moved back to the doorway, his expression hard, set against the sun and the jungle. His leg jutted into the rectangle of searing light which fell in the doorway. Privation had hardened the boyish lines of his cheek and jaw.

"Did you get much information?" I asked Nguyen.

The Vietnamese gave a small smile. "The size and armament of VC units in the area and their direction of march."

"The information could be wrong. The prisoners had to say something," I said.

"Nearly all said the same thing."

"Is it of real value?"

Nguyen was pleased with the question. He licked his chiselled lips gently. He had the face of an Egyptian god beaten out of pure gold. "The value of the information and the fate of the prisoners cannot be correlated if that is what you are trying to do. It has always been that a man can have his life taken for a few coins in his pocket, or for a reckless word." He raised the palms of his hands and nodded at this certainty.

It was nearly 1300 hours and my men were ready to move. They stood silently for once, uncomfortable in their harness, spavined horses, grunts, heads down, edgy, waiting. Then they formed a long single file at the edge of jungle, with Blake's patrol in the lead.

I slipped out of line and went back to the prisoner's hut. The charnel-house smell enclosed me like poisonous gas. Dust settled in the motes of light. The space was empty. I went to the mouth of the big tunnel and was hit by the same stench of corrupting flesh as I stepped into the neatly timbered entrance.

I moved through the passage, flicking on my cigarette lighter. In the half-darkness I was denied the full detail of the scene. The soft corpses of dead prisoners had been dumped in a pile of blood saturated flesh and torn clothing. Half a dozen live prisoners crouched in the dark, roped together, the light flashing on their teeth and eyeballs. I heard a footfall behind me.

"I'm going to get Sergeant Mills to roll a few grenades in here and bring the roof down," Blake said.

"Bloody hell!"

"It's war, Bob. Don't you realise?"

I lowered the lighter over the heads of the live prisoners. One looked like a child, hollow-cheeked, resigned.

"It's war, you pussy," Blake repeated.

In fifteen minutes the two patrols left the huts, moving in a single file along the edge of the jungle. I heard the muffled crump of the grenades. My tongue was like a tainted bladder swelling in my mouth and nausea uncoiled in my guts.

9

At three in the afternoon I estimated that we were not more than perhaps three hours from our own lines at this rate of progress. The thought glowed brilliantly and then died like a worn-out light bulb. What I had seen at the huts had receded to a flicker. The forefront was aching anticipation of death. We were spread out along a track in a shallow valley. We had been moving quickly through the thinnest growth and along watercourses. Then a crack of sniper fire brought us to the ground. We slithered deeper into the undergrowth like snakes.

Blake crawled back along the column reassuring the men. When he got to me, he said: "Charlie doesn't shoot for fun. What does he want us to think?"

The vision of the camp was receding; a few hours away by direct march; but overnight if we had to detour.

"You could call in a chopper," I said.

Blake screwed up his lips in rejection. "It's a cop out. And a big risk for the bird."

"We've got two patrols here."

"That's our strength. Different if we had casualties. What would we say? We wet our pants so we called up?"

Blake and I and the two sergeants leaned our grimy faces together over the map, while our men stared nervously at the menacing thicket of foliage. Blake radiated calm and settled our route.

We inched our way, exhausted, up a low rise through sodden leaves and vines. At the top nothing was clear from the viewpoint. Blake suggested a detour to the south, coolly assured us of the way, and silently directed our movements in the next two hours over the path he determined. For the men the precise way was irrelevant. For them it was mud pools, streams, patches of swamp, banks of slippery creeper and sharp spears of grass which cut like a razor, and spiked plants that buried their barbs in the trousers and pricked through into the flesh leaving inflamed lumps. Every track and bank was fraught with the possibility of landmines and booby traps, and every clearing possibly covered by a hostile machine-gun nest.

We stopped to rest. I conferred with Blake about the route, but it was only formal. Blake said briefly what we were going to do and I had to repeat it to my men. Before we parted I had to speak to him.

"The prisoners you had back there… "

"Yes, Bob?" Blake said gently.

"Christ, Jim, they were slaughtered."

"I did my duty."

Blake used the phrase *my duty* exclusively. He was a professional while I was a volunteer, a graduate of a brief officer training course at a New Mexico barracks. He was an expert in hand-to-hand fighting and infantry tactics, and additionally to stiffen him he carried in his head a knowledge of military history and the philosophy of war. You couldn't devote your life to soldiering unless you believed it was a useful occupation, even a noble one. Duty had to be done.

I wanted to see it as Blake saw it. I was a would-be school teacher, there to help out.

"We couldn't leave the prisoners or they would talk and take arms against us later. That's the reality of it," he said.

"What could the prisoners talk about that would harm us?"

"Every piece of information about us in enemy hands is potentially of help to them."

"Weighed against a human life?"

Blake jutted his chin and moved away. He had undoubtedly allowed me more leeway than he would have given any other junior officer.

We started tramping again and after half an hour we halted near a defined trail. All the men were now convinced that the enemy were close. Since the sniper's shot had been fired we had actually heard nothing suspicious. We had paused a hundred times, frozen by the rustle of a snake or a rat. The rasping of jets and the cough of heavy guns was ominous background music. My flesh crept and my hands shook. We couldn't turn our heads fast enough to fix Charlie's implacable brown eyes.

At the next rest, we withdrew into the bush, drinking from our canteens and chewing chocolate bars. I squatted near my men.

"Do you agree with what happened, sir?" Trask asked. "At Kam Sung."

"Killing those VC?" Moore said. "The motherfuckers got what they deserve."

"They weren't Viet Cong. They were villagers," Trask said.

"They screwed the ass off the woman, too," Schuyler said.

"Yeah. A whole lot of them got into that," somebody said.

"We weren't invited to party," another added.

"What do you think, Lootenant?" Trask asked.

"Get ready to move out," I said.

Maroni turned on Trask angrily. "What's the matter with you, cuntface? Any one of those gooks would have opened your bones!"

"Keep quiet," I said as Blake sidled through the branches like a cat and crouched beside me.

"An hour down the trail," he said with a tight little smile.

"Can we go?" Lucas asked.

"Cleared last week. The nearest thing we have to a main highway," Blake said.

The lure of home was on us strongly now, the temptation to move quickly. Blake rooted out a weed at his feet and drew a plan with his finger in the earth. He pointed to the map and then his plan on the ground.

"We should come out between these two OPs. We're identified. And we're as good as ordering a drink at the bar."

Blake insisted that he speak to all the men. They moved sluggishly into a huddle, pale faces, damp clothes steaming.

"We'll be moving in single file at fifteen feet. Remember your IAs. Watch your nominated flank. Let your buddy behind protect your ass." Blake engaged each man with his eyes and his exhilarating but cold smile. "And remember, men, kill the enemy without mercy. Kill, kill, kill, and God Bless America!"

The words, hissed out very quietly, sent a stiffening charge through all of them.

Soon a chain of men was spread far along the track, moving more quickly than we had all day, tiptoeing, silent as mountain cats. After half a mile we came to a stream and at Blake's signal, slipped into the water waist deep. The stream was festooned with hanging plants and the water clotted with weed. I found a footing on the uneven stone bed and stumbled upstream a quarter of a mile to a point where the channel skirted a clearing.

When I was opposite the clearing sunlight was beginning to strike the water. Hope was expanding with the brightness. Then without warning, gunfire raked along the right flank of the column. It seemed to come from the clearing. Blake's sergeant, Mills, in front of me, groaned and slid under the water.

By the time the next burst of fire started most of the men had found cover under the bank. At first I held Mills' head out of the water. Blood and pieces of bone and slime ran through my fingers. The body leaned on me with such a spiritless deadweight that after a few moments I knew it was lifeless and let it go.

We were pinned down in the water, our ambushers behind a camouflaged earthen rise at the edge of the jungle fifty yards away. Between us was a clearing of coarse grass and fern. I fingered my wet 45 and began to estimate the chance of retreat along the stream bed.

From the machine-gun post came a loudspeaker voice: "Yanks! Surrender or die! Move and we kill you all! Throw your arms on the bank of the river."

The VC voice was American accented, the kind you get by being schooled in the US rather than learned on the street. I could see no enemy on either side.

Blake had made a mistake trying to pass the clearing using the stream, instead of detouring around it in the jungle. Our anxiety to get home had betrayed us.

The loudspeaker voice rang out again: "I prove that we can kill you like dogs where you stand."

Another hail of gunfire cut a thin rope of froth down the centre line of the stream a couple of yards from the men who crouched under the bank. I thought we were safe for the moment in the lee of the bank.

"Throw your guns on the bank and get out of the water. Keep your arms raised."

Silence. The sound of trickling water. The hush of a draught in the trees. Blake inched downstream to me. We spoke with the water at lip level. Blake's eyes were radiant.

"No surrender. We ease downstream. Get into the jungle, encircle them and go for the mothers!"

The order was passed from man to man and a paralysis of fear prevented any questioning. We retreated slowly. After twenty minutes we had jungle on both flanks. The men cautiously eased themselves out of the water through the thick roots at the water's edge. We were under a canopy of trees with a rich undergrowth of swamp roots and creepers. I tried to find a way to mount the greasy bank. Sergeant Mills' body had accompanied my retreat. I grasped the shoulder of the corpse and saw a red-holed cheek and an open eye like a child's marble appear from the amber water. Without emotion I put my boot on the dead shoulder and forced myself upwards through the spear grass and mud to a ledge.

The soldiers, spectres floating amongst the vines, silently reformed and moved back towards the bunker. We were approaching from the rear, inching forward to detect trip wires and landmines. The bunker, a hasty improvisation, was eventually more or less in sight through the trees at thirty yards. I thought we could go no further without attracting fire. The only tactic was to charge, regardless of mines, and try to overwhelm the position.

A moment later a heavy blast of machine-gun fire ripped through the trees near us spraying leaves and moisture from them in the air; it seemed to be a speculative shot. Charlie hadn't seen us.

Blake yelled, "Let them have it, guys! Charge!" and our thin line of men abandoned caution and tore through the foliage towards the bunker in desperation, Blake well in the lead, yelling like a cowboy at a rodeo, a 45 in one hand and a fragmentation grenade in the other. I lurched forward ahead of my men, branches tearing at me. Where the clearing opened out there was nobody to oppose us. I blasted the space with my M16. The VC machine gunner was silent, evidently cut down by our shots. Two Viet Cong rushed from the shelter with their AK47s to forestall the grenades, but were no match for the concentrated fire of our automatic rifles; they hardly had time to raise their weapons. The bunker imploded with a massive shock under our feet as the grenades tossed in by Blake and his corporal exploded.

Opposition suddenly ceased. A striking silence, amid gunsmoke and the acrid smell of exhaust from firearms, a silence again, more profound than before our attack. For a few moments we crouched flat on our bellies in the clearing or in the shelter of the trees, listening, waiting to see whether there would be a counter-attack by hidden VC. Blake crept forward alone. He poked around the bunker. He decided the area was clear. We all got to our feet cautiously, marvelling that we were intact in every limb.

"It was a con trick," he said, as we came forward.

"The loudspeaker made me think there must be at least a platoon of them," I said.

"Three guys! You gotta give them credit," Blake said, admiringly.

I moved the bodies of the pair who had fled the bunker to get a clear sight of them. Young men. Quite handsome. They looked victorious, their cheeks hot and copper smooth, jewels in their eyes. I wondered which one had the American accent.

I turned away, looking above the trees to a few daubs of blue in the sky. I was acutely tired, at the edge of consciousness. I tried to reach back in my mind to all that had happened to us that day. I could remember the grey-green morning hills, with tall moving columns of rain above them. I thought not of the brave men dead at our feet, but of the captives, buried alive in the tunnel, earth in their mouths and blood from their wounds seeping into the dirt.

10

Blake and I moved away from our men while we waited on Route 34 for the truck the US infantry major, who was in charge of the observation post, promised.

"We've had a successful few days, Bob," Blake mused, bright with adrenalin. "Useful intelligence. You're a good officer."

I winced. He was being extravagantly kind. I was a passenger. He didn't mention the dead villagers or VC, if that's what they were, and I hadn't the guts to say, "What are we going to do about this?"

A GMC truck halted. The men gathered round the tailboard, loaded their packs and rifles and clambered aboard. The driver latched the tailboard and climbed into the cab. Blake and I sat up front with him. As we began to bump along the road rutted by rain and traffic, I leaned against Blake's reassuring shoulder. So everything was really in order.

I was jolted out of the haze I had felt since we crossed into our lines. The driver, who looked more like a druggist's assistant with his rimless glasses, drove with verve, throwing the GMC into bends and running up and down the gears to keep the motor screaming. At times the truck slewed, its drive wheels spinning. The most this elicited from the druggist's man was "Whoa girl!" or "Steady baby!"

I turned my attention positively away from the road. To the south, the land levelled out. Many roads had been formed. Bulldozers had scraped away the vegetation. I could see from the windscreen the beginnings of war civilisation. The roads became increasingly busy as we progressed: staff cars, motorcycles, Jeeps, armoured cars, tanks and convoys of tractors towing gun carriages. The roadsides were piled with oil drums. Soldiers laboured over poles and girders. There were fenced vehicle parks, piles of packing cases, cranes, fire tenders, portable bridges. Lines of poles carrying wires followed the roads. Observation towers like oil derricks overlooked the scene. The complicated impedimenta of an army was expanding, creeping forward like mechanical ivy, taking possession of the landscape, leaving raw red dust, tar macadam, concrete blocks, and wire fences.

When we reached our regimental lines, we found that the Regiment had moved to Camp Dakota. We heard that before retiring they had been overrun in a guerilla attack by VC and lost several men. We drove on to Camp Dakota; it was situated several miles from Hoi An on a tract of level land. The bulldozers which had levelled the earth were lined up on the outskirts, rusting. The camp was enclosed in veils of barbed wire which contained a mined space around the perimeter. Inside the wire, the clusters of prefabricated huts were dwarfed by infinite flatness. Few irregularities met the eye at horizon level: a water tower, an observation post, a wireless aerial. The camp gave the impression of being almost unoccupied. A few tiny, isolated soldiers could be seen, and a few vehicles, like beetles, moved over a widely spread network of roads.

At our bunkroom (which I was allocated to share with Blake and Jack Boyd, the quartermaster, as a late arrival) I filled my mouth with white, round, hard candies, crushing them as the sweetness flowed down my throat. I lit a Lucky Strike and tasted the bitterness of the tobacco on my lips. I took a swig of whiskey from the open bottle by the bed, which Boyd had produced for our welcome, and let my mind float freely. I had a quick shower, a shave and changed my stinking clothes.

The Adjutant who had walked up and down the shower room, prodding us along, now put his head in the doorway, sensing our exhaustion. I didn't know about Blake, but I had been on my feet for the best part of seven days. "The General's going to be at the briefing and it's happening now. Transport's waiting. Move your asses, gentlemen!"

As we drove down the road to headquarters, we passed two trucks unloading chairs outside the drill hall.

"Women!" Blake said, appreciatively.

A girl in white shorts with high heels and long lightly tanned legs, a red shirt and a red band around her hair, was standing near the tail of one truck directing operations. The image, so colourful and alien, swamped my grim thoughts.

"Concert tonight. Party from Hawaii," Weston said.

Blake and I followed Weston into the HQ. A female member of the concert party was talking to a clerk. She had her back to me, a long body in thin slacks and a cotton T-shirt. I could see the impression of her G-string panties on her bottom.

I waited with Blake to be called into the briefing room, still damp from the shower, untidy, half-dirty and slightly drunk. The girl was talking to the clerk about trouble with the audio equipment in the hall. Her low, imploring voice made me tingle.

Blake and I were summoned into Colonel Vaughan's office. He introduced Major General Mason from Far East Forces Command. We already knew Major Stuart, the intelligence officer from 21st Div HQ. I pushed my aching feet under the long table, whiskey singing in my head. Blake's mission was the one the General wanted to hear about; mine would be taken in writing as usual, and would be pure fiction, when I had time to produce it. Blake produced his map and made markings on the wall map. He began to explain. Major Stuart made notes, commenting enthusiastically, as though he was a football coach discussing a game. I caught the rich whiff of the General's cigar. Blake described the capture of the tunnel complex and its occupiers as a dramatic enemy engagement. He mentioned only the six or so who were interrogated and said they died of wounds. Nobody inquired further about the deaths. He gave an account of the enemy strengths in the area and their movements, and concluded with a rousing account of our rout of the machine-gun nest.

I walked along the road alone after I left the HQ. I would have to dress later for the scheduled parade, and then I assumed that we would go to the mess for drinks and later the concert and dinner. I wished that I could go to bed. It was cool now; there was a faint breeze. The colours were deepening. The sun no longer burned. The sky was an even yellow. In the direction of the coast I could see grey lumps of rain cloud. I walked past the drill hall. A collection of stage props were piled by the main doors. The dark-haired girl was there.

A soldier was kneeling over a loudspeaker, microphones, amplifiers and wires all round him; it was Trask. He had a screwdriver between his teeth. I set a course to pass close to the girl. She didn't look up at the crunch of my boots on the gravel. Her attention was on Trask's bare back, his curling golden hair newly washed, the dorsal muscles swelling up from a taut waist.

"Haven't you earned a rest?" I said to Trask.

Trask, one hand locked inside a speaker, didn't answer, but swore and groped deeper. The girl headed up the steps for the cool of the hall.

I followed. "All ready for the performance?" I asked.

"Not quite, but come the hour we'll be there," the girl replied in a harsh voice.

"Are you here for long?"

"Just tonight. We're doing all the camps."

"What made you come up here? It's no picnic."

"The money," she laughed coarsely, as though the question was stupid.

I nevertheless felt myself stirring as I talked to her. She had thin lips and tight lines around her mouth, but... "What do you do?" I asked.

"Sing in a nightclub in Hawaii."

"It's just a few nurses here, well mostly."

"Nursing? Not for me, that one. Night duty. Blood."

I gave up probing her for a selfless motive. Trask was now watching me pointedly. "We'll maybe see you after the show," I said.

Trask overheard me. "Oh, sure!" he said. As usual, the officers were homing in on the women.

I walked away unaccountably embarrassed by the encounter. I knew it was trivial, meaningless really. I walked back to my billet and rested on my bunk. I was weak and aching. I seemed to be in the hut at Kam Sung. Outside, the vegetation steamed; inside, the stench and the flies hummed...

I had another shower when I awoke, first hot then cold. I began to dress. The dark-haired woman would be dressing for the concert. Gail would be handling trays of bloody instruments. Maggots would be gnawing the corpse of the woman who complained about the unjust war.

I marched with my platoon to the parade ground. The ranks were opened for inspection. General Mason had long legs bowed inside the narrow blue breeches of a cavalryman. He was tall and passed along the ranks with silent blue lips at scalp level, his head hung benevolently forward. He gave no sign that he noticed the shirt buttons undone, or the lieutenant with one epaulette. He touched his ceremonial sword and moustache alternately with the same hand as he shuffled along. Colonel Vaughan and Adjutant Weston followed the General, but they noted every irregularity, every loose buckle and dirty boot.

Colonel Vaughan barked out the regimental notices, and the Padre said a prayer and a few words about the glorious dead. I was swaying with fatigue. The band began to play the Retreat. The Regiment held a long salute while the flag was lowered. The band massed its noise in the last battle, the last cannon shot of the day; the bagpipes called the soldiers back across the fields with their dead for burial, and their wounded. A drummer, more skilful than the rest, fitted many small pulses into the melancholy beat. The old ceremony of retreat evoked images of broken gun carriages in the mud, and still ribbons of battle smoke in the silence at the end of a day of war. It was an incongruous ceremony, utterly unmoving to me because no modern army stopped fighting at sundown or respected the truce of the Tet; it was the romance of war.

The silver ball of cloud above us cracked open and fat globs of rain began to pound the parade ground. The members of the command group flicked their heads around like cockerels. The Adjutant shouted. The Colonel interrupted. The ranks broke. The men were splashing for shelter in all directions. Colonel Vaughan, seen through a lattice of rain, was standing at attention while others fled. The officers crowded into their mess hut, excited and good-humoured at the sudden relief of tension.

Pfc Trask was waiting, sheltering beneath the eaves of the

officers' mess hut, and he moved forward to intercept me, his blade-like face pale and his eyes staring.

"What is it?" I said impatiently, never pleased to see Trask. We sought a place away from the busy doorway.

"This, sir," Trask said, producing folded papers from his pocket.

Without knowing more, I said, "Can't this wait, surely?" But I took the papers and opened a page of childish handwriting under the heading of Trask's name, number and unit.

I glanced down the page: *On patrol... we joined Capt Blake's patrol... he had taken prisoners including a woman and children...*

"What the hell are you going to do with this?"

"I'm reporting it to you and Colonel Vaughan."

I felt two intermingling plumes of anger and shame rise in me. "What the fuck *for*, man? I can't do anything. It's over now. For God's sake, forget it!"

I had assured myself that I was still considering what the correct action, if any, might be, but I still told Trask to forget it. I wanted time to get my own head straight. It was true; I was searching for reasons which might justify what I had seen with a mind that was feeble. I was confronted with the prospect of reporting Jim Blake's involvement in a slaughter; it was virtually unthinkable.

"What happened was a crime. Sadistic violence." Trask's voice was flat, nasal, unfeeling.

I flinched under his contemptuous stare. "I'll read this more carefully tonight and see you tomorrow."

"Very well, sir," Trask said, saluting. "I won't forget sir. What happened can't be forgotten. And I suppose you'll be making your own similar report, sir. You know what happened."

"I'll discuss it with you in the morning."

11

I couldn't clear my mind and I gave up trying as I pushed through the mess room doors. First, drinks and the pleasant haze of alcohol, then a concert, followed by dinner. Wine. A taste of peace.

Long trestle tables were laid with white cloths. A Regimental shield had been hastily fixed over the bar. The officers milled around the bar talking loudly, their uniforms stained by the rain. Vietnamese mess boys in white jackets carried trays of drinks and oily canapés. There were guests from other units in the camp and ARVN officers. I drifted around the fringes of various groups filling up on pastries and whiskey. When it was time for the show, the rain had stopped and I walked to the hall with Jim Blake and Jack Boyd. An orange moon rested on a silhouette of the jungle like a poster for *South Pacific*. The papers Trask had given me were acid in my pocket. I stopped Blake after a few paces and let Boyd walk on. "I want to show you something." I steered him near to the light coming from the windows of a store, and produced the pages.

"What's this, Bob? Not now surely?"

"You better see this now."

Blake reluctantly eyed the papers. I thought I saw a look of unease, but when he raised his head to the light his expression showed a smudge of amusement.

"This man's an idiot," he said. "He can't take it any further. There's only one way out of here and that's through Vaughan. Vaughan won't listen to this sort of shit."

"I think we should tell Vaughan about it ourselves. Get it squared away."

"There's no need, *Mr* McDade. Tear it up." He walked on.

On the rare occasions when Jim Blake addressed me as Mr McDade it was either meant as an order or a sign that I was being a fool.

"Suppose he writes... " I said, catching up with him.

"All letters are censored."

"Suppose he does somehow manage to make a complaint outside the Regiment? Wouldn't we be best placed if... we had our story straight inside?" I said, hearing my own conspiratorial approach as though I was listening to another person.

Blake smiled slightly, undisturbed. "Alright. If you insist. You're scared, aren't you? An anarchic little scumball private has you by the balls."

Scared? Was I actually scared? I *was* scared, but I had nothing to be scared of. I'd done no wrong. Well, not positively. I'd let things happen... What could I have done? What should I have done? Or to be more accurate, because the issue hadn't disappeared, *what should I do?*

Inside the hall, under the unshaded electric bulbs the officers pushed their way along rows of chairs to get the best view. I sat with Boyd beside me on one side, Blake on the other. Shadows passed behind the curtains, furniture scraped, spotlights flashed, female voices gave inaudible directions.

I saw the dark-haired girl slip out between the curtains to speak to the musicians who were tuning up; double bass, keyboards, guitar, clarinet and drums. She seemed to notice me as she tripped back up the steps and re-entered the curtains, followed by the odd wolf whistle.

Boyd elbowed me and made a gurgling noise. "Lovely little bimbo."

There was a heavy tread of marching outside. The men were arriving now that the officers had taken their pick of the seats.

After a long wait, a slow hand clap and an apology from the manager about the audio equipment, the show began. I drifted along with a series of can-cans, solo songs, monologues, and stand-up comic jokes. I clapped feebly. The girl with the dark hair, introduced as Ann James, apparently one of the stars, wore a green silk off-the-shoulder dress split up to her thigh; the harsh colour jarred, but the material clung to every line of her voluptuous body. She sang a romantic song in a dry, graceless voice. *I'm-in-love-with-you...* The audience were enthusiastic, but probably not about her singing. *Never-leave-me...* The iced overtones cooled my blood. *All-my-liiiife...* The song ended in the discordant catterwaul of her voice and five musical instruments.

We were soon submerged in the crowd pressing to get out to the road. I steered away from Blake and Boyd. I felt bloated and wanted to walk before going back to the mess dinner. I walked slowly, not consciously heading anywhere in particular, and paused under the porch of a darkened hut.

The sound of night creatures from the distant jungle was muted, a blurred screech. I sat on the steps of the porch and wiped the sweat off my face. Gail would be in her room in 'Gon writing letters. The woman of the unjust war would be reduced to an arrangement of bones in heavy red soil. I sat still for a few minutes, half conscious. Then I heard footsteps. A man and a woman. At first I thought of them as an unwelcome interruption. I listened to their separate treads, the undertone of their talk, their sighs. I began to enjoy the thought that they would pass close to me without knowing I was there. The couple walked to the door of one of the concert party billets; they went inside. The lights came on. I was too far away to see through the bright square of window. After a minute the light went out.

I was late for the dinner and I turned back towards the mess. I could summon no more than a strolling gait. The heaviness of the night held me back and saturated my shirt when I tried to run. I burst into the light of the mess. The white-clothed tables were laid with silver. Even in a campaign there was space for the Regimental treasures. The officers were still clustered around the bar and some had become loud and expansive since the concert closed. Vaughan was amongst them, taller than most with bent shoulders and forward-swinging arms. When the meal was announced, Boyd and I had taken seats near the passage that led to the cookhouse, a good position to sample delicacies and wines at the beginning of their journey around the tables.

Before the dinner service began, a procession approached the CO's table, led by a braying bagpiper, followed by the cook bearing a platter aloft, and the mess sergeant behind, bearing another. Vaughan and the General were the first to sample the haggis soaked in Scotch whisky. As the delicacy was served, the equivocal noises from the other diners reflected a forced approval of the delight to come.

In 1945, the 33rd Regiment had adopted, as a gesture of amity, this mess tradition of the 9th Infantry Regiment of the Black Watch, alongside whom they'd fought at Arnhem. Many of those partaking of the dainty, secretly recoiled from the taste of dried sheep's blood and oatmeal broiled in a piece of gut. After a while there was a low call for more, and satisfaction that none was left.

After the chastening effect of the haggis had passed, the conversation flamed again. I could catch the phrases from a dozen subjects around me but no mention of those who had died, including two commissioned officers, when our lines were overrun while I was on patrol. I had no appetite but I chose the curried beef as the simplest option. The walls and corners of the room were shadowed. Faces reflected the white of the tables. Silver and crystal flashed. Talk was subdued by food. The jungle breathed through the latticed shutters. I gulped a Chardonnay from the Napa Valley, juice of America. The lamps in the room fought to thrust away the darkness. The rain started again and hammered on the tin roof so fiercely at times that conversation was overcome. Voices were raised. Agitation showed on some faces remembering what was out there. The spread of food and wine had the appearance of being conjured out of darkness to confuse us. We pressed ourselves against that bright world without being able to enter it entirely. Although washed, combed and uniformed, there was a cramped, creased, unkempt, excluded look about us, like children from a boys' home at a Christmas party.

The General, as guest of honour, sat next to Colonel Vaughan at the head table, the indignant vertical lines of his face contradicting the benevolent nodding of his head. Colonel Vaughan, never a socialiser, sought to create conversation. He called to nearby officers by their first names, sometimes the wrong name. He blurted remarks and interjections to right and left without waiting for replies and guffawed loudly to cover the confusion. Although a spluttering of talk greeted Vaughan's sallies, a silence began to settle over the gathering. We were outmatched by the enthusiastic wind and rain that slapped and racketed around the flimsy building.

Near the conclusion of the meal, to the detriment of our eardrums, the pipe major played tunes inside the mess. His eyes popped and his ears swelled red with effort. Tradition required him at the conclusion of his repertoire to step to the table, utter a Gaelic oath, and quaff at one gulp a horn of whisky, now a glass, placed there for him. The diners were alert to see their piper display his manliness. He threw the draught down his throat and banged the stemmed glass back on the table with such violence that it broke. His belch brought a round of applause as he plunged toward the door, retching violently. Nerves snapped; we shouted with laughter. I would not have been surprised to see somebody leap up on a table and dance.

Later, a hush that may have been disappointment passed over the company when Vaughan announced that he would pass the blue bonnet, another inherited tradition. This meant that he would throw one of our dress Glengarries to an officer who would have to tell a story. The teller then had the opportunity to designate another unfortunate. Every young subaltern had searched his mind for something amusing and not too dirty in case the blue bonnet should find him. The mess rules on formal occasions were that work, women, religion and obscenity were taboo. The painful moment when the CO selected the first victim came. The bonnet was passed and some hesitant and incoherent anecdotes were received with forced hilarity and jibes that sometimes concealed irritation. As was likely, the bonnet came to Boyd who had a reputation as a raconteur. He rose slowly and looked around. He had drunk a lot and swayed, steadying himself on the table. He turned his red face to the roof and grimaced at the rain. We laughed. He placed the too-small hat on his untidy yellow hair. We laughed. He frowned at the audience. We laughed. It was assumed that this was the relaxed preparation of a man who was sure of himself and had something to say.

But moments passed and nothing happened. The audience started to move questioningly in their seats.

"Come on, Jack," Vaughan shouted.

Boyd stared at him in an affronted way. The General looked questioningly at Vaughan. Boyd mimed the General's long face and nodding head. A burst of laughter was quickly stilled.

Boyd was finally pulled down on to his chair by Blake and me. Vaughan appeared to be apologising to the General. The bonnet died out after one more humourless attempt by the Medical Officer.

The time had come for Vaughan to make his speech as CO and host. He must have thought that he had to do what he could to plead the cause of the soldiers before him, to redress the balance in favour of himself and the Regiment, but obviously he couldn't whine excuses in the face of a man who had power over his own future. As I saw it, Vaughan looked frozen in his chair. He had to decide the moment, propel himself to his feet, bang a spoon on a glass for silence, and launch into the void with something that would energise the marionettes. He would see the doughy pallor of the faces confronting him, rows of eyes shining like cheap beads. He would know he would get only artfully concealed scorn and derision, unless...

Vaughan's usually sound memory let him down. He had no notes. He hesitated, appearing to test various phrases. "Engines of discipline" was a phrase he kept repeating. His voice was hoarse and dry and pleading. His attention became concentrated high in the ceiling above the tables. He said he would be avoiding the issue if he regaled them with table talk.

"If we'd fought and lost a battle even with such heavy

losses, we might feel a sense of pride at least. But we were caught with our trousers down. It casts a reflection on me," and here he turned to the General, without adding "And you too, General."

"And gentlemen, it casts a reflection on your competence too. Morale is low. It drifts low in war. We must impose the firmest discipline upon ourselves and our men. Let's make a regiment we're proud of!"

The light patter of applause reflected relief. Nobody communicated with Vaughan when he sat down. Nobody complimented him. Nobody commented to him, not even the General. He sat icily alone.

The rule that the officers could not leave their places until the CO did led some at the outer reaches of the room to slide beneath the tables and work their way out of sight to the kitchen, but otherwise the company waited uncomfortably for Vaughan to signal a close. After a few minutes I heard confused sounds from outside, at once hilarious and angry. The shouting became louder, many voices above the lessening rain. Vaughan looked uncertain. The General frowned. There was a staccato burst of fire from an automatic rifle. My scalp contracted.

The Duty Officer came into the mess and spoke to Colonel Vaughan. The word spread quickly in the room. A riot in the drill hall. A riot? It seemed impossible. Vaughan was still. The diners were held to their seats by the thin string of discipline, waiting for his command.

"We'll adjourn the dinner for thirty minutes. There's a disturbance of some kind at the drill hall. All platoon commanders report there," Vaughan announced.

12

The officers crowded through the mess door; they buffeted each other in the dark outside, curious, enlivened, safe in the assumption that this wasn't a Viet Cong attack. The drill hall was in sight. Soldiers were running out whooping and shouting. Broken chairs were scattered outside the door. A further burst of fire gushed in the air. A soldier brandished a rifle over his head. The men were like drunks leaving a saloon in a wild west movie.

When some of the officers pressed into the hall it was nearly empty. The riot, if that is what it was, was over. The main lights were off, chairs overturned, the curtains torn from the stage, a spotlight flared into a corner. A soldier lay on the floor near the stage, his head bleeding profusely, broken glass sprayed around him. A medical orderly bent over him, dabbing at his head.

Ann James crouched a few feet away, sobbing, US dollar notes on the floor around her. With one hand she was gathering the notes; the other held her torn dress together.

"Hit with a bottle, sir," the orderly said to Colonel Vaughan. The General stood behind him. We could all hear discordant sounds of singing from the road.

It was only when Ann James was helped to her feet, that it became apparent that her reluctance to rise was not the result of injury. Her thin silk frock had nearly been torn off and she had to hold it cautiously around her. Generous parts of her thighs and breasts were visible and she did not appear to be wearing pants or bra. A circle of solicitous officers enclosed her, in no hurry to cure the riddle of her near nudity. Her real concern appeared to be less for her personal privacy than the greenbacks now wadded protectively in her hand.

"They asked me to sing, and somebody grabbed me, tore my dress… "

"What was the money for?" Vaughan asked.

"Singing. The boys had a whip-round."

"What about him?" Vaughan indicated the wounded man.

"Somebody hit him," she shrugged, unconcerned.

"Who?" Vaughan asked.

"I dunno."

"Why?" Vaughan asked.

"The guys had a few drinks."

Boyd passed her his uniform jacket which she slipped into, letting her rag of a dress fall to the floor. She pushed the bundle of notes into a side pocket.

"Oh, thank *you*." She drew the jacket tight around her waist, swung her long bare legs and wiggled her hips, the garment an inch or two below her pudenda. "I feel good in this. I'm a major now, am I?"

Blake and I were well back in the throng of at least a dozen.

"This is the best part of the show," Blake said.

"Vaughan is incandescent," I said.

"Don't blame him. It's bad enough without a goddamn general looking over your shoulder. Mason must think that Vaughan has lost control of the unit."

The talk around us was more about the girl than the event. "Jeez… those tits!" After the injured man had been removed, I saw Vaughan staring at the strange geometry of the bloodstains on the floor.

The Duty Officer had the task of organising a search for the culprit who had wounded the soldier, while the officers returned to the mess hut. We continued the tail of our meal with fruit, cheese, coffee, brandy and wine.

Colonel Vaughan felt he should address us again. The General was on the point of leaving. When Vaughan rose, silence fell with awkward immediacy. I thought Vaughan was concealing his feverish temper, as the faint sheen on his reputation faded in the eyes of the General. Vaughan hesitated. Fragments of a declaration which seemed to be whirling through his mind came out but seemed meaningless. He talked of severe punishment. "In the heat of war," he added, "you have to expect these outbursts."

Vaughan's remarks drizzled away in confusion. He had hardly resumed his seat when there was a shout from outside. The door blasted open. A subaltern riding a black goat charged in. The goat knocked two mess boys out of the way and galloped round the perimeter of the tables; it slipped over, rolling on the floor, smearing its rider with soft green turd from its dirty backside. A mess boy held the door open for the animal to escape, while the rider eased himself up from the floor, smelly and triumphant. Amusement and applause rippled the company, and led, in conversations afterwards, to memories of other after-dinner japes while we waited for the Colonel to depart. When he had gone, we left in ones and twos, drawing an aura of cigarette smoke with us into the humid air.

I stood outside the mess in the bars of light cast by the slats in the shutters, listening to the pock-pock of diesel compressors, the grinding of trucks hauling supplies, and the whirr of air conditioners. The jungle had receded, the insects were stilled. I felt awake now and stifled. I decided to go back to my quarters via my platoon's huts to see whether the hunt had been abandoned. As I approached the huts I could see interior lights, and Sergeant Lucas standing outside. There were signs of activity down the entire line of huts beyond those that housed my platoon; a few lights, the yellow pencil lines of flashlights, the shine on a face or a hand. The search went on.

"Found anything, Sergeant?" I asked.

"See for yourself," Lucas said, leading me inside.

As I entered, a chorus of moans greeted me.

"These shitbirds are more drunk than awake, Lieutenant."

Lucas used a flashlight to supplement the dim light bulbs and indicate a man in the corner who grinned when the beam was held on his face.

"What are you doing, Trask?" I asked.

"Waiting."

"Get into bed," I said, feeling I was addressing a child. "It's long past lights out."

"No, sir," Lucas said. He said to Trask, "Get your boots on." His torch fixed on a bloodstained shirt on the floor by the bed. He shone the flashlight on Trask's cheek, revealing scratches and bloodstains.

"Just a moment, Sergeant," I said, signalling that we two should go outside.

I had more or less settled in my own mind that there should be no reprisals for tonight if I could help it. I didn't want to feed Vaughan's flame. Lucas faced me squarely outside, his protuberant eyeballs reflecting the light from the porch. I could hear his breathing.

"If you want to leave him until tomorrow morning, sir, it's alright by me. He'll have had a shower by then and soaked his shirt. What do you think he's waiting for now? He's expecting to be arrested. He's guilty and he'll confess. But he'll be harder to nail tomorrow. And we won't have any witnesses out of this lot."

"Why are you turning him in, Sergeant?"

"Because he's an asswipe. A screw-up in the squad, and out there he's a fucking menace."

I considered. Trask was truly useless, manifestly in revolt. I didn't want to cross Lucas, the disciplinarian of the platoon. I couldn't afford to ignore his advice. Lucas would be loyal to me only up to the point where his own reputation and efficiency could come into question.

"OK," I said reluctantly and waited while Lucas fetched Trask and a two-man detail to march him.

Trask, looking resigned, was marched into the darkness.

13

I walked back towards my quarters. The sky had cleared. The breeze had dropped. Stars prickled through the cushion of heat. I stopped outside the QM Store where Blake and Boyd were still talking, passing a bottle of whiskey.

Boyd had uncovered the authorised version of the evening's events and was explaining them. "She wasn't singing, Bob, well, not a lot," he said, passing me the bottle.

Boyd honed his story in the retelling. "What happened is quite simple. She was persuaded to do a strip act. The boys put a few bucks in the hat. There was about thirty of them. They were loaded. They went into the hall and took over. On with audio and spotlights, off with the roof lights and with Lady James' clothes. I guess they were having a good time until she put her muff too close to one of the tigers. The rest you know. They never hurt the girl. An unlucky asshole got whacked with a bottle. Good clean fun."

"She said her dress was torn off," I said.

"She couldn't say she'd taken it off, could she? And she nearly didn't get her bucks. That's what I said to her afterwards, when I was rescuing my jacket. She hadn't got any organisation. Let me handle it, I said. We'll have a clean, well-run establishment. We talked it over. She and a couple of others were willing to turn a trick or two."

"You're pimping for them?"

"Ugly word, Bob. The girls have rooms, somebody to arrange customers, and somebody to keep an eye on them in case anybody gets rough. It's a public service. Nobody's worrying about lights out tonight. It's time to be happy. Tomorrow is hell."

I had the hot impact of whiskey in my guts, smoking up through my lungs and throat. I wished the pair goodnight and decided to go to the mess bar.

A few officers were left haunting the bar. Vaughan had returned unusually, brooding over a cognac. The General had retired. The Medical Officer was discussing the wounded man. "These wounds are never so bad when you clean them up. Stitched up like an old boot. Disfigurement? Nasty scars but nothing compared with the work of fragments of a landmine or a grenade, eh?"

The MO surveyed the plump fingers that had so nimbly stitched the old boot, and then picked up his glass and tossed it off. "You can't imagine the advances surgery can make in a war zone. Cut and stitch. Lateral thinking. Save a life. Back home there's a sodding lawyer with a writ for negligence leaning over your shoulder."

Those who were listening stared, unamused. Peter Weston, the Adjutant, came in and spoke to Vaughan. Vaughan said loudly, "Good work. Gentlemen, we've got the sonofabitch who committed the assault tonight. He's under lock and key. I'll deal with him tomorrow." Vaughan fanned his wall-eyed grimace across the assembly. "Now, who's for a game of cards?"

The four or five who agreed to play began to arrange seats around a table. Two decks of cards appeared. A green felt cloth was placed over the table. The players took seats, removing their stakes from their pockets and placing them on the table. The bartender placed chosen drinks at their elbows. The game began, that eminently private and unsocial circle of grunts, nods, sly eye movements and terms of art that is the game of poker. I remained on a bar stool, whiskey in hand, bored but still unnaturally alert, watching. It was nearly two o'clock when they declared the last hand.

There were thirty dollars in the pot, which Vaughan opened with a bet of a hundred dollars. Everybody except Blake threw their cards in. Blake had to decide whether to pay a hundred dollars to see Vaughan's cards, or even raise the bet.

"See you," Blake said, dropping a hundred dollar IOU on the pile. He spread his own cards without waiting: two pairs, aces and twos.

The others whistled, but Vaughan looked exultant, a line of sweat shining on his upper lip. "Full house. A pair of jacks and three threes," he said, throwing his cards face down into the discards.

"Show," the Medical Officer said, reaching over to grab the cards before they were shuffled into the pack.

Vaughan was raking in his winnings with one hand, and reaching for the discards with the other. "What's the matter with you?" he snarled. "You never played the hand!"

There was a silence at the table. I could hear the bar steward gently arranging bottles behind the bar. The MO growled drunkenly, and reached out for Vaughan's cards again. Blake's hand came down on the MO's wrist. Blake quickly drew all the cards together, face down, shuffled them briefly and laid them in the card box.

14

I walked down the road from the officers' mess with Blake. The moon was high, chased by a few clouds. The stars had gone. Machinery was grinding in the foreground while the jungle breathed in the background. There were few lights on in the camp.

"You didn't press to look at Vaughan's cards?" I asked.

"He probably had the cards, Bob. Have you thought what would have happened if he didn't have them? Our commander unmasked as a cheat. What would that do for morale?"

I looked at him. Blake thought like that. The integrity of his commander was worth more than a hundred and thirty dollars.

We were approaching the Quartermaster's Store, which was still lit. A soldier came out and disappeared into the darkness.

"Boyd's still in business," Blake said.

We looked inside and Boyd saw us. "Guys, you've got time for a bit before you go home. Last customers, only seventy-five bucks. Blonde or brunette, take your pick."

"I'd like to make it a perfect day," Blake said. "A fight, a drink and a fuck. Blonde for me."

"Come on, Bob," Boyd said.

"Not me. I'll have a nightcap," I said, sitting down and grabbing the whiskey bottle on the table. I had the stench of Kam Sung in my nostrils. What I wanted was oblivion;

I would sort out my head tomorrow.

Blake and Boyd went further into the hut and in a few minutes, when Boyd returned, he attempted persuasion again. I refused the offer but went on taking shots from Boyd's bottle, talking stupidly, sitting with the chair propped up against the wall... until I passed out.

I drifted into consciousness slowly. At the end of the store, past the piles of shirts and jackets, tins of paint and the smell of rope, was a small sleeping compartment. An electric cord ran from the ceiling to a shaded bulb near the head of the narrow bunk bed. It threw harsh wedges of brightness into the room, leaving the rest in shadow. A head of dark hair shone under the light.

"You're the Loot who talked to me before the show," the girl said with a grating laugh. Girl was the wrong word. In the light, she was a woman of thirty.

"How did I get here," I croaked.

"Your friends dumped you."

She stood over me wearing a black bra and a red thong. Her eyelids were lowered, hiding the eyes; there was an odd touch of gentility in the inert face, but she was actually an abrasive, high-mileage whore. She bent over me. One breast slid out of the thin bra.

"What's your name, feller?" she asked.

Without answering I sat up slowly, swung my legs to the floor, and fumbled for my trousers and boots, which had been dumped there.

"You're going? It's all paid for. But put that on," she said indicating the condom on the ammunition box by the bed. She pulled off her pants, slipped out of the bra and lay on the bed confidently. She put her hand on my shoulder and tried to pull me over towards her. I continued dressing and struggling for sobriety.

"What did you say?" she asked tiredly, after a minute.

"Nursing. The patients were too much for you?"

"Did I tell you that?"

"This afternoon."

"The things I say. Shit, it wasn't the patients. It was me. Caught in bed with one."

"Did the guy mean anything to you?"

"It was a woman."

Her arm had fallen away. She was on her back, in the past. "I hate bedroom confidences," she declared.

"Tonight at the hall didn't worry you?"

"Naah, I'm used to it."

"That's rough company."

"I can look after myself. I don't want a fuss, see? This job's worth plenty to me. If AE knew I was making bucks on the side I'd be back in Hawaii so quick it wouldn't be funny."

"We've arrested a guy."

"Oh, yeah. I don't want to know."

"You know the guy?"

"I haven't a clue. Look, I don't want trouble. I don't think we want this either." She snapped the overhead light off. "Have we finished for the evening?" she giggled.

"Let's say you've earned your money, if that's what you mean," I said, pulling my boots on in the half-light.

"No more work tonight," she said sleepily.

The reservoir of lust beneath my skin was low. Her body was hot, greasy with sweat, and stank of the men who had had her. I tried to trace my way back to the morning, to yesterday, where I had lost the trail… A nerve vibrated in the back of my neck, causing a sharp pain. In the darkness, the eyes of the prisoners caught the light, terror-white…

15

I was awake, steaming, bell chimes dying inside my head. The sky, through the small window, a vat of molten lead; the air choked with whiskey, decaying vegetation. Capes and jackets hung on the walls, cramping the space.

Blake and Boyd lay on the other two beds as naked as I was. Boyd was on his back, snoring, cast like a fat sheep, gut trembling. Blake's face was hidden in the pillow; only his fair hair showed.

I sat up, retrieved a pair of crumpled denims from the floor and wriggled into them. I put my bare feet into my boots, picked up a bowl, a towel and my toilet bag and went out the door. I yawned, stretched in the heat haze, and walked towards the showers. A few keen men were about. Two sergeants passed me, shaven and slick. I went into the empty washhouse. As the warm water from the shower streamed over my skin I could see the broken woman.

I heard the tread of official boots and Peter Weston's modulated tones. "Not ready yet, Bob? You may have to charge your man, Trask. There are two other suspects too. We'll work out who's responsible. The Colonel will hear the charges at ten-thirty."

"Vaughan's being unreasonable. He's got a lot of command problems. He wants somebody to vent his fury on."

Peter Weston said, "Look, we've always turned a blind eye to a bit of drinking in barracks, but if there's going to be fighting and criminal violence we've got to show the men where they stand."

Weston was stiff, unremitting, neat as a cadet at military academy. I grunted a tardy approval into my towel. I saw my face in the shaving mirror. A road map. I rubbed the lines with my forefinger: laughter lines, sun lines, stress lines – not age, surely.

"You look bloody awful, Bob. What were you drinking last night, kerosene?"

I wondered why Weston was hanging around. I lathered my cheeks, heard the crash of the sea on a Maine beach and then smelt the rotten smell of the tunnel. Weston stamped around and came closer.

"There's something I want to see you about, Bob. It concerns this man Trask. He's handed in a written report to Colonel Vaughan about an incident on patrol. Gone over your head. Killing of villagers. Murder."

I could glimpse Weston's incredulous and worried face in the mirror. "Yeah?"

"He names Blake as in charge, Nguyen the liaison officer, Blake's sergeant Mills, who was killed, and two corporals. What do you know?"

I continued shaving. What I should do had been turning uncomfortably inside me like a lump of indigestible meat. "I read the report."

"What are you or were you going to do?"

"I don't know."

"What happened, Bob? Is this a smartass move by Trask to get involved in something which will take him outside the line of normal duty? You were there, for chrissake!"

I continued scraping and avoided Weston's urgent glance in the mirror.

Weston waited a few moments. "Yeah, maybe you ought

to keep quiet. We'll take it a step at a time. Report to Vaughan's office in an hour. I'll see you there."

Weston marched into the light and I could hear him unleashing his frustration on two unlucky privates slouching on the road. He could be at his desk until 3am and yet prowling the lines at dawn to see that the men were smart and moving to schedule.

The others were awake when I returned to the hut. Blake, sitting cross-legged on his bunk, was using an electric shaver. Boyd was sitting up, his hands clasped around his temples. Both of them fixed me with red eyes.

"Have a tasty piece of pussy last night?" Blake asked.

"Thanks for picking up the tab," I said, "but you could have saved yourself. I was juiced. She went to sleep. I staggered back here when I came to."

Boyd stiffened up, unbelieving. "You're a wanker! We'll get a refund."

"My girl had the hottest ass in Christendom," Blake said. "What a great end to the day." He shook his head, reliving the pleasure.

I completed dressing; short-sleeved shirt, lightweight trousers, webbing belt. "I'll get over to the lines to see how the liquor search is going."

"Pouring it out, that's the heart-rending part," Boyd said.

"Vaughan comes up with some diabolical ideas," I said.

The men were on parade outside the huts when I arrived. They had been ordered to form three ranks outside *as they were*. One wit was naked. Dazed and groaning they stood in untidy ranks of T-shirts and underpants. The search details worked through the soldiers' possessions in every hut, but as they became bored with the task, the tempo increased. Instead of being felt, kitbags were emptied on the floor, mattresses rooted up, clothes strewn about. Unsympathetic fingers plunged into every packet and pocket. Nests of bottles were dislodged from their caches and carried clinking into the daylight. The men watched wistfully as the pile of bottles increased: gin, whiskey, rum, vodka, cognac.

"The liquor is forfeit," the captain in charge announced, "and will be poured out now. If you had liquor in your possession we have a note of it and you will be charged."

With perverse grins the corporals began to open the bottles and pour the contents on the ground.

A dispatch rider approached on a motorcycle. He followed the road rather than use the flat earth, which meant that he went two hundred yards past the parade, turned a right angle and came down our road like a child playing a game. Inaudible words with the captain followed.

"Get on with it," a sergeant said when the pouring slackened.

"No," the captain said, "the Colonel has decided that the rest of the liquor will be confiscated."

A muffled cheer broke out.

"Silence! You'll be charged just the same and you won't get it back!" the captain shouted. "Dismiss!"

"Fucking Army doesn't know what it's doing!" the captain said to me.

16

I strolled through the cookhouse supervising the C Company breakfast. I passed by black ovens with sausages swimming in vats of gravy, fried eggs by the hundred, the cooks in dirty white jackets tossing their pans, ignoring the intruder. As soon as I bent to look more closely at a platter of bacon or a tray of bread, the process required that it be snatched away. The mess room was an open-sided shed vibrating with the rattle of plates, curses and shouts. The lions were feeding and best left alone.

A soldier poked a plate at me: a lonely half-sausage and a squirt of gravy.

"A morning's work on this, sir?"

"Get another helping," I replied, signalling the nearest steward.

The steward dismissed the soldier with the gentle malice of authority. "No more. None left. Guys tucking into three and four."

"Get him something else. Fried eggs, bacon. Something."

"It's not an à la carte restaurant, sir."

"Get it."

"He's too late."

"Get it. That's an order."

The steward slumped away to comply. The soldier remained looking at me with curious disbelief for a moment, and then resumed his seat with his cronies; they shared frowns, darting eyes, uncertain why the anticipated failure of their buddy's request hadn't happened.

I kept my appointment at Regimental HQ. Weston told me that Vaughan had not arrived that morning, and he assumed we were supposed to be at Vaughan's quarters. We walked there. At the door we met a Vietnamese servant with a tray of tea; misunderstanding military protocol he gestured us to step inside. When we did, we realised that Vaughan was still in bed. The blinds were drawn; it was unusual. Vaughan was often about before reveille, although it *had* been a late and drunken night. The servant approached the bed, announced us and proffered the tea tray.

"Whaaat?" Vaughan said, exploding upwards in the bedclothes and knocking the tray to the floor.

The orderly scuffled on the floor picking up pieces of crockery. Vaughan watched with a screwed-up face and then shouted, "Get out!"

"Reporting as ordered, sir," Weston said.

Vaughan never replied. He threw off the bedclothes and climbed out, hairy and spider-like in his pink pyjama pants. He pulled on a navy-blue spotted silk dressing gown, went over to the washstand and sluiced his face with water. He dried himself, puffing hoarsely, and turned his attention to the uniform laid out precisely on a chair.

I looked around. Meticulous was the word. Hair brushes and bottles of lotion on the dresser, a clock in a leather case, books on a stool beside the bed, folded shirts and ties on a shelf, rows of shoes beneath. Though occupied scarcely twenty-four hours, it was the room of a finicky bachelor.

Vaughan did not attempt to dress but combed the cropped grey hair on his head unnecessarily. At last he deigned to notice us. "Why are you here?"

"I understood we were to meet and discuss this report about... an event in the field... on Mr Blake's patrol," Weston said, handing him a copy.

Vaughan began to read without any reaction. "Trask says he handed you a copy, Mr McDade. What have you decided to do about it?"

"I was still thinking about it when Peter told me you had a copy."

"Yes, you can leave it to me. You must realise, as I do, that this is a damned lie by a yellow commie sonofabitch who'd do anything to get out of the heat!" Vaughan's eyes dulled as he appeared to contemplate the Regiment's involvement in war-crime killings. "We're not going to let this maggot even start a story like this, we're going to squash him like a bug. My God, our lines overrun, a riot in front of the General, and now a fucking allegation of a massacre! The first thing the Army will say is, 'Vaughan's finished off the Third'."

Vaughan tore up the notes and dropped them in the trash can. "This isn't going one inch further, gentlemen."

Weston and I were silenced, and then Weston said, "This man Trask is one of three picked up for questioning over the riot."

Vaughan's good eye sharpened. "Is he?"

"We don't know whether he's the guy who wielded the bottle," I said.

"Oh, but he is *involved*." Vaughan paused to see if we were following his thoughts.

"Well, sir, we'll have to see... " Weston began.

Vaughan's colour was changing from a cheesy pallor to lined redness. His voice had an edge. "No, Major Weston, we won't see. Mr McDade will deliver Trask to my orderly room with appropriate charges. I'll get it out of him. By the time he's had thirty days in the stockade in Guam, he'll have paid his dues for last night, and his fairy story about a massacre will have been knocked right out of his skull."

Vaughan smiled slightly at the neatness of the solution. "I think I've solved our problems, gentlemen. Dismiss."

17

Torn paper in the trash can. Would that end it?

The rain began. I drew my cape around my shoulders and let the water wet my hair and run down my neck. I walked silently with Weston and parted from him knowing what I should do. I should return to my quarters, write a full report on the patrol and formally ask Colonel Vaughan to carry out an investigation. I should just do that, and let it all go to hell and take me with it, if it must. At least then I would be able to breathe. I would have rid myself of the fever breeding inside me. Maybe Vaughan would react as he did a moment ago: accept Blake's view that he was carrying out a legitimate interrogation. Of course that is what Vaughan would do, and perhaps that would be confirmed by other witnesses. Vaughan would impede the calling of many witnesses. He would claim operational necessity. He would make sure Blake's story was backed up by Nguyen. If I knew the men of my patrol, never mind Blake's, none of them would testify against Blake, his men, or Nguyen. The old mantra 'Don't know nothing about it, sir,' would apply.

I reflected, my eyes down, kicking the wet gravel on the tarmac. If I reported what I knew, my friendship with Blake would be destroyed, and my future with Gail. How could there be a future if Gail's lover crucified her beloved and heroic brother? However much my report was found to be truthful and justified, I would surely be a leper in Gail's eyes. And I would be boycotted by my fellow officers. No comrade in arms could be as evil as our enemy, the fanatical and virtually subhuman Viet Cong who blew our balls off with their mines, and drove us into madness. I would be a pariah. And if the events in my report were followed through and found to be factual, Blake could end up in prison, discharged in disgrace. And a vital – it seemed vital now – part of my own life would be laid waste in pursuit of… what? A kind of abstract justice.

And who *were* the victims? They might have been the hated VC, as likely as not to die in battle. Perhaps it didn't make much difference that they had their throats cut. Or were the victims intimidated or half-innocent villagers, aiding and abetting the VC? There were children; were children always innocent? Surely in all this land there were many simple people who lived and died cropping and fishing, and if there were, those whom Blake ordered to be killed may have been innocent… It all swirled before me in a turbulent flow.

I rolled my cape over my arm. The rain had stopped. Steam was rising from the hot ground. In the past, in the moments when my imagination wasn't making me fearful, Vietnam seemed so attractive; the harshness of the weather, and the harshness of the Army bearing down on lives. Now, I yearned for the peace of wearing any old clothes and going to the supermarket unshaven… having a conscience that was clear and shiny as a mirror.

I hitched a ride to the guard house on a truck. Feeling queasy, I had missed breakfast. My eyes watered as I scanned the arid spaces of the fort from the cab of the truck, blind sheds and little anonymous khaki creatures scurrying like beetles. Tentacles of lightning grasped the low clouds. My ride dropped me at the guard house compound. I argued with the sentry in a cloud of diesel smoke from the departing truck. I didn't have a pass. A misty rain began to fall on my shoulders.

I pulled my cape around me roughly. The sentry was dry in his box. The guard corporal was dry under the porch of the building inside the wire. The rain intensified. The sentry yielded and let me into the compound.

"Darrel Trask," I said to the corporal. "Hearing at ten-thirty today. I need to see him. Prepare charges."

"You haven't got a pass, sir?" the corporal said. "I have to have a complete record." He pointed to a thick book, eyes swelling behind his glasses.

I pointed to my wristwatch. "I'll lose an hour going back. There's no time."

"Sorry, sir."

"That's it? Oh, shit."

"I can't help you, sir."

"Get me your boss on the phone."

The corporal paused, looked at the intercom handset on the table, his eyeballs roving behind the glasses. "Well… OK, sir," he said, standing aside to admit me.

I followed the corporal down the cell corridor. "No smoking, no matches, no gifts, sir," the corporal said.

Trask, stripped to the waist, lay on a bunk. He did not look up as I was let in. I sat on the cover of the lavatory bucket and leaned back on the mesh door.

"Make yourself comfortable," Trask said, swinging himself up and around into sitting position. He was a fit man, wide shouldered with a thick muscular neck and a narrow blade-like head. The comic book he had been reading fell to the floor between his feet.

I threw a pack of Camels and a box of matches on the bed.

Trask was enlivened for a moment. "You're a real bolshy, aren't you? Breaking all the rules. Whaddya want?"

"I have to prepare charges against you."

His rough fingers extracted a cigarette from the pack; he had a miserable boy's face posing as an adult's. I knew his personal file. Army convictions for assault, disorderly behaviour, drunkenness. A hardball. Yet a relatively good head. A clean civilian record. Qualifications as an electronics technician. A man the Army hadn't tamed.

"Don't ask me for help. I'm innocent, I am. Yeah." He spun himself back to lie on the bed looking at the ceiling, as if to underline a resolve to admit nothing.

"There's the shirt, and the marks on your face and hands."

"And is the shirt mine? You better find out. What can you prove?"

"The girl."

"Slut." He jerked up on his elbow, his eyes wavered, perhaps sliding back to the memory of her. He fell back. "She can't identify me because it wasn't me. As for the cuts, I slipped off the catwalk backstage last night, bits of metal and bolts sticking out everywhere. Got me as I fell. You won't get anywhere."

"The guy that got cut is in bad shape."

"You're making me cry, copper." He pointed derisively to the raw trail of the scar which crossed his own chest.

I pitied Trask, but the man was determined not to help me or himself. "You'll need to get your witnesses together. I can see them and do that for you."

"Yeah? You're going to help me? What kind of a sucker do you think I am?"

"There could be more charges."

"Whaddya mean?" Trask said, jerking up on his elbow again.

"The girl. Indecent assault. Or assault with intent to rape." I didn't think it would get this far but I wanted to give him a shock.

Trask's face flattened. He was at bay, hair pricked up. "I never touched the bitch. You charge me with what in hell you like! Do your damnedest!"

I got up to go hesitantly.

"Oh, and one thing Mr McDade, sir, don't forget my complaint about mass murder. I haven't forgotten. You were there Mr McDade, sir. You saw. You're railroading me because of my complaint, aincha? I know. Fuckin' Army!"

18

Weston and I went to see Vaughan at HQ.

"We're in difficulty on the assault charge against Trask, sir," Weston said. "Mr McDade has established that Trask denies it and there's no other evidence."

Vaughan exhaled a long breath of exasperation. I looked at the two framed photos Vaughan had placed on the shelf by his desk. One showed him as a subaltern, a German prisoner of war; as now, thin to the point of emaciation. The other photo was a picture of an old woman with a family resemblance, genteel and proud.

"I can hardly believe it! We have casualties, we're overrun, and when I'm trying to explain it to the brass, we have a brawl under our noses! The General thinks the unit has gone to hell. If that isn't enough, we have an evil little grunt alleging a massacre! I'll be damn lucky if I'm not recalled. Bring the sonofabitch to the barrier! He'll scare."

"But, sir," I said.

"What about the injured man?" Vaughan asked, ignoring me.

"Concussed. Didn't see who hit him," Weston said.

"The woman?"

"I understand she doesn't know anything," Weston replied. "She'll have gone now. Her party were pulling out at first light this morning."

"Do I have to do everything myself?" Vaughan groaned,

his head with its wall eye gyrating. "*Has* the woman gone? Stop her! Bring her to HQ immediately!"

When we left Vaughan's office Weston detailed a staff sergeant to find Ann James.

In twenty minutes she was outside Vaughan's office.

"What's all this about?" she asked me, while we waited in the general office.

"You told me you couldn't remember who the guy was who was making free with a bottle last night."

"Yeah, right."

"You need to tell the Colonel."

In the hustle of the office Ann James appeared to simmer. The clerks couldn't take their eyes off her, her brightly coloured erect figure, outlined breasts, nipples pressing under her T-shirt, and the sickly sweet perfume.

Vaughan called Weston and me in. "Have you talked to her? No?"

"Well…" Weston began.

"Good. I'll do it. Then we call Trask and get her to identify him."

"Wouldn't it be better, sir" I said, "if she was asked to choose from the group of others who have been implicated?"

"Jesus, mister! This is the Army, not the fucking FBI. Bring her in!"

When Ann James was shown in, Vaughan unusually and awkwardly stood up, but it was a formal politeness without charm. "I know you want to get away, Miss James. I'm sorry you've been troubled. But I'm afraid we had a serious breach of discipline last night and men have to be charged and punished. We've got the man we're certain is the right one. We want you to confirm it."

"Uh-huh. And if I can't?"

"In that case you won't get away today or tomorrow or even later. I'm determined to find out who did this, and you're a material witness. Do you follow me, Miss James?"

Ann James nodded miserably. Vaughan asked Weston to bring Trask in.

"Is this him?" Vaughan asked her.

Trask, a large figure in a small space, quivered like a fractious horse, his head rolling on his pylon neck.

Ann James hardly seemed to glance at him. "Yes, that's him. Sure."

"Fuckin' liar!" Trask shouted.

"Shut it, soldier!" Weston barked.

"Hear that, Mr Weston and Mr McDade? We have identification."

I thought I ought to intervene, but if I did I'd have to explain my conversation with Ann James, when and *where* we talked… In a few seconds the opportunity passed.

"March out the accused," Vaughan grunted with satisfaction.

I followed Ann James into the outer office. "Can you wait a minute? I want to talk to you."

"I haven't time," she said, slipping elegantly down the steps and beginning to walk back towards the drill hall, her ass wriggling energetically and her sling-backs clacking on the road.

I caught her up. "Listen, you told me… "

"What a woman says in bed is one thing."

"Christ, we were never in bed. Not in the way you mean. This is serious!"

"So's my job." She stopped, faced me. We were alone together in the oven, sweat on our faces, suffused by the smell of her, like a choking gas. "Are you trying to make trouble for me?"

"Trask is one of my men. I want to see he gets a fair shake."

"You ought to train your men better. I'll tell you. I saw him after the show. Before I was in business with Major Boyd. He paid me, and afterwards the sonofabitch took the money back and nearly broke my arm! He's a shithead. He deserves all he gets."

"He may be a louse, but that doesn't mean… "

"Yes it does. It might as well have been him. Now I'm going."

I caught her arm. My fingers sank into her flesh. It didn't *really* matter if I told Vaughan and Weston where I was when she told me she couldn't identify the attacker. I was just pretending to be good. "No, you're coming back with me."

"Get off!" she shouted, shaking herself free as a Jeep skidded to a halt a few feet away.

"Tut, tut, mustn't squeeze the fruit," Boyd laughed.

Ann James hissed private words for me alone: "If you insist, I'll identify that bastard again, *and* tell your Colonel that you were drunk in bed with me. It won't look so good for you!"

She strode away, thighs quivering as she stamped her feet.

"Wassamatta Lieutenant?" Boyd asked. "Take a ride. You didn't get any last night. Kinda too late now."

I collapsed in the passenger seat. "She's a treble A bitch."

"She's an Alakea Street whore. What do you expect? What you got with her this morning anyway?" Boyd said distantly, easing the vehicle forward. "Nice little show last night, wasn't it? Wonderful ass."

19

The Regiment was resting. There was talk of being back at the front in two weeks. 'Training' was underway, a refresher for an experienced bunch, enough to keep motors tuned. I visited the various sections where my men were occupied; gun and mortar drills, jungle craft, grenades and landmines, survival skills, first aid. I watched without interest, hardly listening. I was conscious of the minutes ticking by and made my way back along the road to HQ when I was sure the charges against Trask would have been decided.

I met Weston in the squad room, face to face. He had a handful of files and turned away, anxious to move to another job. I pursued him. "What happened, Peter?"

"Ninety days' hard labour in a high security unit," Weston said, without emotion.

"Bloody hell!"

"It's history," Weston said, beginning to talk to one of the clerks.

I came out of HQ into the road almost into the path of a passing Jeep. I rubbed my face with damp hands. I began to walk, my boots jarring on the tarmac, the toe caps glinting in the sun, my hatband compressing my skull into an ache. Trucks laid a thick trail of fumes past me. I gulped blue air.

An Australian Army Jeep stopped near me. "Want a ride, Yank?"

"Vehicle park?"

"No problem," the driver said accelerating fiercely. The Jeep fishtailed on loose gravel.

"I wish we could take off!" I yelled.

"I'm trying, mate."

As I climbed out of the Jeep at the park, I saw Blake talking to the driver of a GMC with a trailer; it was the entertainment party's wagon, and it moved off when I was twenty-five yards away and came past me. Ann James was seated in the front smiling, next to the driver, no doubt looking forward to her next engagement, the footlights, the applause, the money.

"She couldn't care less," I said, when I reached Blake, indicating the disappearing truck.

"You mean Lady James? Why should she?"

"She identified Trask so she could get away, and he got ninety days' hard."

Blake pulled me into the shade between two trucks. "Why are you getting in a friggin' knot about this punk Trask? We throw men into stinking mud-hole combats that nobody will ever hear about or care about, so why bother about this guy?"

As I understood Blake, human life was the fuel that was burned in the war machine; individuals were meaningless. As long as the conditions of the military were sustained – discipline, unity, and strength – and the machine was annihilating the enemy, the cost in friends or foes didn't matter. War for him seemed to have a kind of beauty, a deep satisfaction, and to fight was the rationale of his life.

I shrugged my shoulders without confidence in the face of such certitude. "The guy is one of my men. He didn't do the bottle attack."

We walked to the gate of the vehicle park. Blake gathered

a folder of papers from the office at the gate. "No rides. Let's walk," he said.

I had the inferior feeling of the amateur talking to the professional when I was talking seriously to Blake about things military. "Vaughan has shut Trask up and buried his report," I insisted.

"So what? Very wise I'd say. Trask's a no-good sumbitch who wants to get out of the fire. He'll get his wish – in hell. I know where I'd rather be," Blake smiled.

"You think nothing will happen about the report? I saw Vaughan tear it up myself."

"Nothing. Weston told me. Vaughan won't wear it," Blake said lightly, unconcerned.

"But… people know."

"You calling me a killer?" Blake said with a grin, but with tense lines around his eyes.

It was a crucial moment and I hesitated at first, and then said in a low voice, "Hell, Jim, you're a hero of mine."

It was an utter lie. I was behaving like a craven coward and I knew I was. I knew Blake didn't mind me regarding him as a hero.

"It was a legitimate interrogation, Bob," Blake said more softly.

I recovered a tiny speck of my guts. "About ten or so people, including children?"

"Three hundred if fucking necessary!"

"I don't know, Jim. Explain it to me."

I was still grovelling.

"You know, you dick-head. Our lives would have been endangered if we had left them."

"That's not interrogation."

Blake stopped and faced me, his lips only a few inches away, pink, with shiny white teeth and a pleasant breath, bearing in mind what we'd done in the last twenty-four hours; a faint, distant humour at the corners of his mouth.

"If you want to make something of this take it to Vaughan yourself. Tell him. He can't have thought anything of the report. He hasn't even mentioned it to me himself. But if one officer says he has evidence of killing by a brother officer, Vaughan will have to listen to that. If you really want to shit on the Regiment and on me, do it, man!"

Our eyes were locked: Blake's bright, challenging; mine quivering, blurred.

After a pause, Blake punched my shoulder playfully but hard. "You're a good guy, Bob, a serious guy. Gail's lucky to have you."

We walked together without speaking. I thought Blake would go on killing with warrior lust, shoving aside the corpses, from major to colonel to brigadier to general, and on to honourable retirement. I was half a step behind in understanding, half soldier, half civilian, perhaps half man. I could be looking for a job at twenty-seven. Handy with mortars. Passable with a pistol. Leave out map-reading. A useful man in a chocolate factory. The Vietnamese woman in the hut had a face that was flattened with silent pain.

The darkening clouds squeezed down on the jungle. We ran the last few yards to our quarters, saturated.

Boyd was reclining naked on his bunk.

"There ought to be a law against bodies like yours," Blake said.

The rain roared and cooled the air. We three were comfortable and intimate. We jawed idly. Blake seemed to have dismissed my remarks as trivia; we were still making eye contact, conversing on subjects a world away from the bloody crotch of the unjust war. We joked. We were buddies.

20

Weston looked tired. His hands shook slightly. Some of his papers were scattered on the floor of his office. The fan whirred monotonously and created waves of warm air. He was working on a small cleared space on the desk-top, wearing a pair of steel-rimmed glasses. He looked unsoldierly compared to his immaculate toy-soldier appearance when he was marching.

I stood in the doorway. Outside, the anti-room was crowded with soldiers. Clerks kept pushing past me, asking Weston questions. He was performing several tasks at once.

"Can I speak to you alone for a moment, Peter?"

Weston took no notice. He went on instructing a clerk. When the clerk went out I stepped in and closed the door.

"Couldn't it wait till tomorrow, Bob?" Weston said tiredly. "I've got a lot on at the moment."

"It's about Trask."

"Urrrrggh! History!"

"I want to see Vaughan and try to persuade him to drop the charge."

Weston's face tightened, the narrowing brown eyes searched the corners of the room for an answer. "Whaaat? You've got no chance! What's got into you, man? You wouldn't understand what it's like having to work with Vaughan. He won't hear you, Bob… he fucking doesn't listen to *me*!"

"I need to try."

"He won't listen to me, Bob. I've had more weird problems with this guy than… "

"I need your advice Peter, off the record."

"Wait a minute. I'm not giving you any immunity! Nothing is off the record. I'm an adjutant, not a stress councillor."

I hesitated, and then decided to go on. "There could be some truth in Trask's allegations about the killings. I was there."

Weston's expression curdled sickeningly. "*Could be?* You were fucking there. Don't grease me with *could* be. It's true or false."

"We're all screwing up sending a man away for something he hasn't done, to silence him."

Weston removed his glasses. "I'm not going to ask if you were a witness to what happened on that patrol. I don't want to hear about your involvement."

"It would be in everybody's interest, including the Regiment, if Vaughan investigated and sent the real culprit down on the assault charge, and then conducted an inquiry into Trask's report." I had finally reached the point where I should have been twenty-four hours ago.

Weston threw himself back in his chair and waved away a clerk who tried to enter. "This would involve Jim Blake. Probably the best officer in the unit, gazetted to take over D Company in a month, and probably the whole bloody Regiment in a year. Your friend."

"I don't want to hurt Jim, but… "

"If anything bad happened on that patrol, killing villagers, Vaughan will be finished. What do you expect him to do but try to close the can of worms?"

"He's found a lousy way."

"Hell! It's gone too far now," Weston said, standing and

placing a calming hand on my arm. "Why take this line, Bob? OK, so you don't agree. You don't like it. Trask's your man. All that. But why stand out against the old man when he's absolutely determined? You can't achieve anything, and you won't do yourself any good."

"Let me see him."

We found Vaughan striding restlessly around his empty desk. The room was large, quiet, shaded from outside by low trees. Vaughan bade us enter cordially, looking from one to the other, the movements of his head excessive because of the wall eye.

"Well, gentlemen?"

Weston said, "Mr McDade wanted to raise a matter in relation to Darrel Trask." The downbeat tone of his voice and his immediate departure from the room suggested that the matter was unimportant.

Vaughan was coldly quiet for a moment, probably anticipating my concern. Then he smiled. "We've finished all that, Mr McDade. The man is scum. He's got to take his punishment. We *have* to make an example of him."

"I know the man's completely innocent."

"Don't say another word, Lieutenant. What's done is done."

"Trask has raised a serious case of what amounts to a war crime, and you're putting him away to shut him up."

Vaughan coloured, stood up and raised his voice. "He has no credibility. He's a louse. I've given him a light sentence. He could get five years in a state pen for what he did."

"He didn't do anything. The woman was lying because she wanted to get away with the entertainment group."

Vaughan came close to me and squinted suspiciously. "Whose side are you on, Mr McDade?"

I could smell an old man's caried breath.

"There's other evidence of what happened on the patrol, and surely it warrants investigation."

Vaughan was distracted and looked out through the shutters at the rubber tree outside, swaying in the wind.

"Other rats?" he mused. "It doesn't make any difference at all, except to strengthen my resolve to put Trask somewhere where they'll kick his head up his ass. Nobody else is going to come forward are they? Nobody else is low enough to rat on his unit."

Vaughan turned round to look lopsidedly at me, braced, shoulders back, legs wide, arms hanging from his shoulders, loose-wristed.

"I think, sir… "

"Enough, Lieutenant. Dismiss!" Vaughan said, resuming his seat.

I stood my ground.

"Dismiss, I said!"

There was a long silence. The sunlight through the trees outside dappled a square of floor, reflecting on patches of water that still lay on the tiles after the daily mopping.

"Mr McDade, I gave you an order, which you have ignored, and now I'm going to give you another. As Trask's CO you will march him on parade at sixteen hundred hours and read the charges and punishment to the Regiment."

I found my words undeniably there, like stones in a gear mechanism. "I can't do that, sir."

Vaughan's lined face now had a bruised darkness about it. His fingers hopped like small monkeys from article to article on the desk, touching each, placing them precisely and passing on, the notebook, pencil holder, calendar, paper weight. "One more opportunity for you, mister."

"Don't force me to be involved, sir."

"You could be court martialled for this."

I remained silent. Vaughan rose from his desk, came around to me, staring closely into my face, breathing heavily and twitching. Suddenly he raised a hand and pushed his fingers between the buttons on my shirt, crumpling the material and securing a fistful, which he twisted.

"You will, by God, you will!" he shouted.

I put my hand on Vaughan's chest and pushed him away. Vaughan let go of me and teetered backwards, slipping on the damp tiles, twisting to try to save himself a heavy fall. His head struck the side of the desk with a crack and he flopped on the floor.

The door behind me opened. Weston was there with a clerk. They rushed forward and helped Vaughan to his feet. Vaughan was stunned, unable for a moment to stand unsupported.

I was numb with shock myself and I stood still.

"Take this officer into custody," Vaughan muttered.

21

I was placed in a large vacant quarter by the parade ground. Weston was with the detail escorting me.

He was like a man in pain, eyes wide, lips drawn back. When the detail had been marched away leaving us alone, he said, "You're not to attempt to leave here without my personal permission. Agreed?"

"Yes."

"What the fuck have you *done*, Bob?"

"It was an accident. The old man grabbed my shirt and I pushed him off... "

"Yeah, yeah, but seeing him in the first place. I tried to tell you!"

I brought the palms of my hands up hopelessly.

"Where's this going to go? What's a court going to lead to? Have you any idea?" Weston said in a thin, hysterical tone.

He would have to mastermind all the paper work and deal with a fractious commander.

I grimaced. "Do you think Vaughan might cool down?"

"No I don't! Not the way it happened. Witnessed by me and the soldiers in the office. The story will spread. He can't let you get away with it, Bob. You're a complete jerk. You've started something now that we can't stop. People are going to get chewed up. And we have a war to fight! Oh, shit!" Weston went out and slammed the door closed.

I sat down on a chair and lit a cigarette. I could see it vaguely, a momentum in events that was more than the contribution of all of them. I felt more distressed than humiliated or angry. I asked the Vietnamese servant who came in to dust the furniture to get me a cup of coffee. The drink seemed to require an inordinate amount of fussing from the servant when it came. When I gulped a mouthful I scalded my lips.

What had happened with Vaughan made me think that the life I had imagined with Gail after the war was now at a further remove. I don't know why I should have connected the two but in my fears there was perhaps a buried connection. That future life had always been distant, the product of sleepless nights alone in my bunk. It was attractive, but always glossy and flat like a page in *Vogue* magazine. Marriage, children, a home; coming home at six in a business suit, or tweeds if I was teaching, mowing the lawn at weekends, taking Gail to a baseball game. A kind of unattainable domestic perfection.

I could look out across the parade ground towards the network of roads beyond. Convoys of vehicles were crawling across the barbed wire landscape. Bodies swayed in the back of trucks, squeezed together, helmets at angles, clutching their weapons. Trask kept bobbing to the surface of my thoughts like Mills' corpse in the river. And the Vietnamese woman, the stretch marks of old pregnancies on her white belly.

I saw Weston walking towards the mess for the afternoon break, his normally upright head was down. I could see a change in him. He had lived with the model of the warrior for years and once aspired to be one. Now the Army was fast ceasing to lose its fascination. He had lost his stomach for war, the relentless pressure and the sheer disfunction of it. He wanted to be home with his family, preferably in a quiet administrative post at Fort Montgomery, because he still loved the Army in the abstract. He was yellowing at the edges like an old sheet of paper. He would make half-colonel and eventually a steady desk job but he was no longer a man with a future like Blake.

Officers were approaching the mess building from all directions, some walking, some being driven. Blake arrived ahead of Weston. The cook would have made a fresh batch of muffins or cookies. The smell of baking would be like the smell of 2nd Avenue, Saratoga Springs on Saturday morning. The officers would fetch their coffee or Coke or orange juice, and gather together as the word spread. *An officer from 3 Comp was to be court martialled.* What *for*? And *who* was it? McDade? No. Yes, it *was* McDade, a mild guy who was a big buddy of Jim Blake. The air of amiability which the comfort-eating of muffins and biscuits generated would be tinged with excitement about the news. Weston, always assumed by others to know everything, would probably resist the whispered questions. Amid the upsets of war, the court martial of a brother officer was yet another wacky event, and quite insufficient to inhibit the appetite. Four or five singed and broken biscuits in a constellation of crumbs would be all that was left as the officers put down their coffee cups, patted their bellies and made ready to return to their duties.

I watched the parade from my window. The Stars and Stripes, raised at reveille and lowered at retreat, hung from the flagpole in the still air like a dead bird. The parade ground and the roads and buildings beyond it seemed a long way away, and they quivered in the heat rising from the surface. The Regimental Sergeant Major, energetically stiff and shining, spaced five soldiers across the ground. The companies of the Regiment and the platoons within the companies were formed up on the road in a long column of threes, awaiting the order to march on. The men, standing easy, moved restively to make the best of their last freedom before remaining stone-still for half an hour.

An order, and the Regiment banged to attention. The column marched on to the ground led by Colonel Vaughan, swinging arms raised high, paddling through the air, each company peeling off on its marker. The solitary tapping of a drum gave precision to the left footfall of the marchers. When the whole Regiment had halted on the parade ground, the RSM's shouts moved them into straighter rows; the scraping of boots on asphalt was like a roar whenever he moved a file of men a few inches to left or right. I could see Trask and his escort waiting on the road. A huge balloon of sullen grey cloud had drifted to dominate the scene. Now they were ready, the officers lined behind the Colonel, facing the Regiment. To one side, Trask and his escort, also facing the Regiment. Colonel Vaughan began to address the assembly, but at this distance I could only guess what he said.

22

"That's the story," I said.

Amherst wiped his palm over his skull and sipped the whiskey. "The essence of this is that the facts are trivial although the charge, striking a superior officer, is serious. Should never have been brought. Vaughan should be a better man manager than he is. In a theatre of war the court only wants to try grave cases."

"So you can get me off?"

"Nothing guaranteed, but, yeah. I reckon you have a good chance to get away with maybe a reprimand at worst. We need the girl, James. Show she was mistaken, in a hurry to get away."

"What makes you think she'll admit a lie, call it a mistake?"

"Nothing. We'll have to see. If she's helpful we'll use her."

I didn't voice my uneasiness about Ann James. It wasn't specific; more a feeling of mistrust. "What about Trask's report?"

Amherst flicked through my copy. "Crudely written, but graphic. It will probably lead to an official enquiry, but that's another matter. This is what was animating you, and it explains Vaughan's cover-up." He took a deep pull on the whiskey, savoured it. "I think it's crucial."

"Am I likely to be asked about the allegations in the report?"

"Sure. You're named."

"But Jim Blake and Gail… "

"The Court won't want to hear *too* much. Another cartload of muck on a mud-spattered Army. You'll be on oath. It happened."

"I could say… I don't *really* know what happened."

"I don't read lessons on morals, Bob, but my advice as your lawyer is to tell it how it was."

I was momentarily ashamed of showing myself as a pliable would-be liar, and I returned to Ann James. "I'd sooner we did without her. She's not reliable. She's a whore. Her first loyalty is to herself."

"And yours?" Amherst's grey eyes were as opaque as stone.

"OK, ok, ok!" I said, grabbing the whiskey bottle and pouring a draft down my throat.

"I know what you mean about James," Amherst spoke dismissively. "She's hard, used to looking after herself. It doesn't necessarily mean she won't be of use to us."

Amherst slid his papers into his briefcase. It was the first real tension between us. He said more softly, "I'll see James if she's in 'Gon, and we'll make a decision."

23

I had placed two deck chairs with a striped Coca Cola sun shade stuck into the earth between them, on the small enclosed grass patch outside my quarters. A rubber mattress lay in the sun and near it a towel, sunglasses, a packet of Lucky Strike and a small gold lighter engraved with my initials, which Gail had given me.

I pulled off my shirt and lay in the sun for a time. The sky was a pallid blue with wisps of cloud. I tried to imagine that the sky was the cold sea of the US east coast, but at the same time I was conscious of moving inexorably towards... a kind of chaos. Yes, there would be military men moving around, talking, referring to pieces of paper, but behind this for me, bolts of emotion that would strike me and sear my flesh. I was sick with apprehension.

Gail's voice came from inside the quarters. "Hullo! You're out there?"

"Waiting for you."

"Let me get you something," she said.

I heard the snap of the refrigerator door and the hiss as she punctured two cans. She appeared in the garden with a tray bearing beer and glasses, wifely even in this billet.

"Come over here out of the sun," she said, setting the tray down.

I sprang up, kissed her lightly and fell back in a deck chair. I pressed my hand to one of the cans and felt the numbing cold. "Busy?" I asked.

She drew a line with her finger through the drops of moisture condensed on the outside of her glass, her usually pale face slightly red. "It's been an awful morning. I shouldn't talk about it." Her capable theatre-sister hands, square and scrubbed, squeezed the glass with determination.

"Tell me… it might help me." She was going to tell me anyway.

"We had three Navy boys in today. One for an emergency op. They flew a surgeon in from Guam. He actually spoke to me in theatre as though I was a human being."

"You're more than just a human being."

Even a doctor in this wilderness would have to notice. She had changed now into a light tan uniform skirt and shirt, and shaken out her long copper hair. No sign of the nurse other than in her attitude.

"Bob, you know I thought I'd seen everything violent that can happen in my job – the casualty wards at home with people smashed and cut and burned. I thought that's the way it was in our crazy lives. But war is *different*."

I wiped moisture from my face with a forearm and gulped more beer. I ought to have stopped her.

"War is different because these men with broken bodies have trained for it. Injury is part of the game. The guy that had the big op was a flier, a captain, probably a clever man. And a good-looking one. This is what all his work and study have come to."

"What's poetry or Picasso beside the mystique of controlling an F4 Phantom?" I sounded callous because that was the only way I could deal with her thoughts.

"He'll never fly again. He'll be lucky if he lives."

"What happened to him?"

"He lost one leg at the ankle and another at the groin."

The words hit me in my own groin. "No dick, eh? It spoils things." I couldn't take this talk.

"When's the hearing? I can't stand this," she said, covering her face momentarily with her hands. Her diamond engagement ring looked thin and dull.

"A week or so, then the trenches. A preparatory pounding with artillery before we go in. Back to business." I tried to sound casual.

"You'll get off?"

"The lawyer says so."

"You don't seem all that confident."

"I'm not."

"What happened, Bob? It's not like you to get into a dust-up with authority."

"I had an argument with my CO, we grappled and he fell badly. I suppose I lost it, just for a millisecond. Pushed too hard."

"Uh-huh. Want to tell me what it was about?"

"Just Army shit. A man of mine was being stitched up on a serious charge and I thought I had to say something."

"Jim said in a letter that you were sick, battle fatigue. You ought to see a doctor."

"It'll happen. Part of the trial." Her resort to medical science for the solution to problems irked me. "Maybe Jim's sick."

"Why on earth do you say that?"

"Oh, we're all slightly crackers or we couldn't do what we're doing. I mean, if you saw this from Mars, and you were asked whether you'd like to participate, I guess you'd say, 'No thanks'."

She gave me a glassy, unbelieving look as though I might really be ill. I was thinking the same about her. She was certainly overwrought, and that was understandable. She picked up the tray and went inside and brought out salted cashew nuts and potato crisps, and more beer. In her capable, domestic way she had taken over.

I waited patiently for her to come to what she wanted to say. We chewed and sipped the beer.

"I'm going home, Bob." Her voice was tremblingly casual, her eyes downcast.

"Do you think it'll rain again today?" I asked, grinning.

She laughed quickly, tears poised on her eyelashes. "I mean it. I love nursing but I can do it anywhere. I've done my stint here. I'm entitled to go. The braver the boys, the more I cry. I can't take much more. This is no place for cry babies."

"If you feel like that, you should go," I said, slipping out of my chair on to my knees beside her. Her disturbed lips were close to mine. I touched the soft wave of her hair. I kissed her; she was unresisting but inert.

She pulled away to look at me, saw – no doubt – the yellowed skin, the wrinkled eye sockets, the bloodshot eyes, and she must have seen something more. "I don't know how I'll bear to leave you."

"I'll write a lot," I said, pressing close, but she pushed me away good naturedly.

"We better talk," she said.

Then there was a knock at the door; it was a servant with a plate of cold chicken and salad – my lunch. The servant offered to bring more food when he saw Gail, but we refused. Gail arranged the salad on two plates.

"What's it all about, Bob?" she asked, as she worked at the bench, her back to me.

The clattering of plates and cutlery disturbed me. I was silent. She looked round.

"Are you ill?"

"Maybe."

"Your judgment about what you're doing is all to hell."

"Maybe."

She reached out with the blue earthenware coffee percolator in her hand, absently trying to find a place for it on the gas jet, and it overbalanced and fell, shattering on the tile floor, spreading coffee grounds, water and fragments.

"You need treatment, Bob."

"I don't see any way out… "

"I don't own you, but I have some claim on you. Oh, what's the use! That's why I'm going back. If it hadn't been for you I'd have gone back months ago," she sobbed.

I put an arm round her shoulders and led her to the couch. She collapsed full length and I lay down beside her. She had lost her bloom. She was still attractive, but she wasn't a young single girl anymore. The war had used up the girl, and she was a woman. I felt her stir against me and we made love.

When we broke apart afterwards we thought our separate thoughts in silence for a time. Then Gail showered and busied herself with the food. As I showered I thought I didn't want to surrender Gail to anybody else; a personable surgeon from Guam or Hawaii perhaps. Instinctively I wanted to possess her; it was like not letting anybody have a piece of your property, a self-centred and ultimately painful thought.

Gail, wearing my towel robe, was sitting on a deck chair in the garden and staring at her salad when I came out in boxer shorts to join her. Her expression was hidden by mirror sunshades. I picked up my plate and sat beside her. I was hungry. The lettuce broke crisply in my mouth. The chicken had a coriander sauce. The food here was better than the officers' mess and Gail had a way of dishing it up.

"You've done magic with the cook boy's work."

"I still feel the same, Bob."

"I'm sorry if I seem confused, Gail… because I am. We're

going to get married when I get out of here."

I still clung firmly to this intention; it was the star which had guided me for nearly two years. Except to be heavy with the cowardice of my behaviour at Kam Sung, I hadn't evaluated where Jim Blake stood, and might continue to stand, in my life. I'd shied away from thinking about it, and that allowed me to avoid thinking about where Gail stood. Gail and her brother were perhaps inextricably connected.

"You had to help this man of yours."

"There's a limit… my own army career could be… "

"What's a career alongside the consequences of war? And you face those every day, Bob. Maiming and death."

24

On the afternoon of the case, which was due to start at fifteen-thirty, the miserable figure I saw in the mirror startled me: the long-nosed face with its filmy eyes and the vertical channels on each side of the mouth. I eased my fingertips through the fine spray of silver hair at my temples. I was ageing by the day.

I could hear the footfall of more than one person coming down the corridor towards my room. I took a last glance outside the open window and heard the babble of the clerks across the garden. I had become familiar with their routine. I knew when the head clerk was in the room with them, when they had their tea, when they were preparing to go home. I knew how they reacted to jokes and horseplay, and I could even distinguish the voices of a couple of the leading personalities, all without having the slightest idea what they were saying.

There was a sharp rap at the door: the escort. I was marched by three military police – it seemed excessive – to a spacious stone building near my quarters, standing amidst unkempt lawns. The pitch of the roof swept low over a verandah which ran around the outside of the upper floor. The corner ends of the gables were decorated with carved wooden serpents in faded red.

I was taken to the upper floor. The folding doors were open. The yellow walls inside the vast room were peeling. Two fans turned tiredly in the high-raftered ceiling. The planks of the polished wood floors were hollowed with the tread of many feet. A long bench spanned a dais at one end with six high–backed chairs on it. In front, at floor level, were smaller desks for the clerk of the court and a shorthand writer. Two lines of benches for counsel faced the dais, and behind them a legion of bamboo chairs for the audience. The building was an old structure which had absorbed the contests of many courts and councils.

Amherst, sitting over his papers, smoking, noticed my uneasiness and watched with his crooked smile. "A bloody awful place. Better in an army hut. Sitting up on that bench you get the idea you're God, instead of an officer having an easy day."

I didn't respond, uncertain who the man beside Amherst was.

"Colonel Vale," Amherst announced, gesturing.

Vale turned from his papers and nodded, a minimum of recognition for a brother officer who was, after all, innocent at the moment. He appraised me vaguely from behind his spectacles. He stood up, moving to exercise himself a little. I had expected a tall, satanic figure; instead I saw a short, plump, elderly man with a wisp of grey hair which became unusually thick and curly at the sides and back. He had a nose which had expanded to push his small eyes further apart, giving him an elephantine look.

The court orderly draped a US flag on the wall behind the bench, and laid out pads and pencils. He disappeared through a door to the rear and I had a quick glimpse of a smartly uniformed figure with silver hair. I quivered. He was one of the men who would try me.

Amherst motioned me to sit. "This will be a court of five officers with a military judge to deal with legal issues."

"Very high-powered. Who are they?" I asked, simply to become engaged.

124

"The Judge is Henry Talbot, an experienced former Mississippi court of appeals man. He'll direct the other five. The President is Nathan Aramson, a pen pusher in 3rd Army Supplies Div. Done a lot of courts. Very fair. The others I don't know. It's really a question of availability. But you're in safe hands."

The air quickened. Uniformed officials began to come in and take seats. The Prosecutor's assistant brought a pile of law manuals. The shorthand writer settled in front of her machine. I looked out of the open door-space across roofs of faded orange tiles, and the topmost foliage of trees, towards a spacious purple haze... freedom.

The orderly came through the door behind the bench. "Silence! Stand up for the Court!" he shouted. He was followed by the members. The Judge swore in the members, and the President swore him in, and they took their seats. The members of the Court looked almost amiable. A young major and an artillery captain seemed bemused at the austere surroundings. I could feel the curious gaze of all of them. I wiped the wet palms of my hands with a tissue.

Amherst dug me in the ribs. "Your turn now. Make it good. It's all they'll hear from you for a while," he whispered.

I stood on the orderly's command, identified myself and heard the charges read; assault on a senior, failure to obey a lawful command and conduct prejudicing military discipline.

"You understand the charges?" the orderly asked.

"Yes."

"How do you plead?"

The word 'guilty' jumped into my throat involuntarily, choking me as I tried to speak. "*Not* guilty," I said, as boldly as I could.

25

Vale stood to make his opening statement, flipping casually through his papers, and then putting the folder down on his bench and stepping out into the space before the lawyers' benches. I thought he was trying to give the impression that his case was so simple that he required no notes.

He spoke quietly of the role of a fighting unit in war, the exhaustion, the inevitable and tragic loss of men, the sapping of morale. I leaned to one side to see the effect on the main members of the Court. Amherst whispered, "He's standing between me and the President so the President can't get any idea what I'm thinking, but of course that's a trick that works for me when my turn comes."

"The low state of morale is shown by a brawl which broke out," Vale said, "and a soldier was seriously injured with a broken bottle. The culprit, Darrel Trask, was identified by an independent witness, charged by the CO in his orderly room, and sentenced to ninety days' detention. Trask was a member of the accused's platoon. The CO ordered the accused to read the charge and punishment at a Regimental parade as a very proper marker that violent behaviour would be met by severe punishment. The accused refused, violently punching his CO Colonel Vaughan in the chest. Colonel Vaughan fell to the floor, striking his head."

My already feeble confidence ebbed as Vale spoke. I began to think that Amherst's buoyancy was misplaced. Amherst was scribbling, his mouth tight with concentration, and then he said in an aside, "It's about time I broke this up. Vale's getting too pally with the Court." He moved out in front of the benches beside Vale, apologised, and asked, "Is the Court going to hear from Major Weston and Ann James in support of these events?"

Vale retorted testily, "Captain Weston, yes. I don't see the need for Ann James."

The President smiled. "I'm surprised a woman enters the picture. Tell me more."

Amherst snatched the initiative. "Ann James is the entertainer who identified Trask, sir. Later she told Mr McDade that she had done so only to avoid being delayed in getting away to her next engagement."

"And that's why McDade refused the order?"

"Exactly, sir. McDade tried to persuade Colonel Vaughan that a mistake had been made."

The President nodded and looked both ways along the line of members; they too were nodding their understanding.

Vale growled and barged back into the limelight. "She's not material. She identified Trask in the presence of both the CO and the Adjutant."

The President conferred with the Judge and then said, "I think James is material and you'll have to present her for cross-examination at least, Colonel Vale."

Amherst sat down, satisfied with the effect of the skirmish. "That broke up Vale's opening nicely," he said out of the corner of his mouth.

I had listened to the exchange with misgiving. "You've decided to call her?"

"Not necessarily, but I've spoken to her. I'll tell you later."

Vale called Colonel Vaughan. The CO advanced nervously between the rows of chairs. His hair had been newly cropped and the grey hairs were lighted by his shiny scalp. His uniform jacket with its medal ribbons hung on him loosely. He had lost weight. He jerked around in the witnesses' chair waiting for questions. Vale took him carefully through the riot, the investigation of the assault, the identification by James, the punishment imposed on Trask and my alleged assault on him.

Amherst stood up to cross-examine. "Is McDade a reliable officer, Colonel?"

"Up to the time he assaulted me."

"You asked him personally to investigate possible charges against Trask?"

"Yes I did, or Captain Weston did."

"He told you before the charge was laid that he doubted Trask's guilt?"

"He said there was no direct evidence, but then we got the girl to identify him."

"He told you Ann James was lying or mistaken?"

"I was present. Her identification was very positive."

"But he told you?"

"Yes."

"Why did you go ahead?"

"I'd seen and heard the girl. I thought he was just trying to swing it for one of his men. It was a very serious disciplinary situation."

"Wasn't there another reason why you wanted Trask put away?"

"No," Colonel Vaughan frowned and looked around innocently.

"Hadn't Trask complained to you about the killing of some villagers by a patrol?"

"Baseless allegations by a coward."

"You didn't want an inquiry into a possible crime which might reflect badly on the unit?"

The members of the Court were alert and leaning

forward in their chairs, frowning. An orderly room squabble had veered off into dark matters.

"I tell you the allegations were baseless and any investigation would have found that."

"Putting Trask away silenced him, or at least cast a doubt on his credibility about the killings?"

"That wasn't my intention."

"Court martialling Mr McDade also silenced him about the killings because he wanted an investigation, didn't he?"

"Just a moment, Major Amherst. What precisely are these allegations?" the President asked impatiently.

"I was just coming to that, sir." Amherst held up my copy of Trask's hand-written complaint. I could see that Amherst was in full possession of the case, and Vale sidelined, as tortuous alleys he didn't know existed opened up. But I was disturbed at being portrayed as a proponent of investigation.

The document was admitted in evidence despite Vale's objections and copies were made for the Court.

"Is this a copy of the report from Trask detailing the deaths of twenty-four villagers?" Amherst asked Vale.

"Yes. A slur on one of my best officers by a troublemaker trying to evade front-line service."

"Very well, Colonel Vaughan. Let's come back to your orderly room on the day. Mr McDade will say you left your desk, stood before him, balled his shirt up, insisting that he participate in the parade. It was only then that he pushed you away."

"I never touched him. He punched me."

"You were sitting. How did McDade get close enough to hit you?"

"I was on my feet, standing in front of him."

"Why?"

Vaughan hesitated. His wall eye veered around the room. "I wanted to… emphasise my order."

"You were angry and you put your face close to Mr McDade's to emphasise?"

"Not angry."

"Really? You couldn't give your order from behind your desk?"

Amherst looked at the members of the Court. I could see that they were imagining an angry man. Amherst's expression was one of cynicism and he turned as if to sit down. And then he swung back to the witness again.

"By the way, Colonel, a small point. I take it you agree that your office had recently been mopped and the floor was wet?"

Vaughan assented miserably.

Amherst sat down and leaned across to me. "I doubt Vale will re-examine. He's got his man's story out. He'll keep quiet about Trask's complaint at this stage because it surprised him and he'll want to think about it."

As Amherst predicted, Vale did not re-examine. Vaughan left the witnesses' chair stooped and looking bewildered. The President announced an adjournment until the following morning.

"A first-round win for us?" I asked Amherst when the Court had left the room.

"I think so," he said with his crooked smile. "Vaughan seems to have doubts about what he's done, and the image of authority stands or falls with him."

26

Amherst walked some of the way back to my quarters with me, the escort MPs trailing behind out of earshot.

"Tell me about James," I said.

"She's prepared to say she acted hurriedly wanting to get out of camp. She thought it over later and realised Trask wasn't the attacker. Her evidence justifies you. I think you could be acquitted on her evidence."

I had my head down, eyes on the flagstones, considering. "It's a gut feeling. I'd sooner she wasn't called."

"Her evidence is clear."

I nodded reluctantly.

"Don't worry about the girl. All we want her to do is to tell the truth. She can protect herself adequately by saying she had no idea of the seriousness of the charge or she'd have taken more time and trouble."

I could only express my unwillingness by silence. I was speaking about feelings. Amherst wanted logical argument. I parted from him and the escorts marched me into the building.

I had a shower and changed into a T-shirt and shorts. An orderly brought my supper, a heaped plate of curry and rice. I fetched two cans of cold beer from the refrigerator and sat at the table. I soaked the yellow rice in the curry sauce, filling myself, not thinking of anything but the pleasure of eating and washing the food down with cold beer. Afterwards, bloated, I lay on the bed and went to sleep.

It was dark when I awoke. I was wet with sweat. I dropped

my clothes on the floor and showered again. I didn't think of the case but remembered the curry. The cook must have been interested in food to learn the skill and do it so well. I came out of the bathroom and saw a woman standing in the bed-sitting room with her back to me. I hadn't heard her come in, but she heard me now. She didn't turn.

"Are you decent?" she asked.

"No." I took a clean vest and shorts from a chair by the door and put them on in the bathroom.

When I came out Ann James was rudely moving about the room examining articles, a book, a photo, my watch, restlessly. "You're comfortable for a man in prison."

"How the hell did you get in here?"

She sat down on the bed and began to idly turn the pages of a US Forces magazine. "Sweet talk," she said. She grinned and went on flipping the pages.

"What are you doing here?" I asked incredulously.

"I've been summoned. First, I had your man Amherst at me. Now I've been summoned. Look, I don't understand why you got yourself into a mess over a rat like Trask."

"I had a duty to try to help him."

She shook her head. She couldn't comprehend my remark. She traced a design on the blanket with a long lacquered fingernail.

"You shouldn't be here. Why'd you come?"

"Curiosity. I never thought you were such a twat."

She twisted from her small waist and replaced the magazine on a table by the bed. "What am I supposed to say in court?"

"Tell the truth. You were mistaken."

I noticed now how sexless her face was, lips too thin, nose too long and sharp, eyes too small. With her foxy expression she seemed mean.

"That lets you out, does it?" Her rough voice was cutting.
"It helps… "

She stood and stepped toward me impatiently. "And I get torn to shreds!"

"No, you can explain… "

"I've got a lot to lose!" She came threateningly close, staring.

I moved my head slightly in understanding.

"My job, that's what! If the Army decides I'm trouble, I'm out!"

"This can't affect your job."

I sat down on a chair. Her restless movement disturbed the heavy air. I could smell powder and sweat and see patches of damp on the pink cotton sweater.

"Tell your lawyer friend I'll be the worst witness he ever had! I'll be saying Trask *was* the man and I never told you anything different!"

"God knows, I never wanted you in the court!"

"I told you, the Prosecutor's subpoenaed me. I gotta go or have MPs chasing me. I gotta stand down from my work and be around for the trial. You've got a hell of a nerve, buddy. You want to be a saint, and you want me to jump on the barbeque with you. What kind of mouse are you?" Her nostrils flared with temper. She spat a gob of saliva at me.

She picked up a rod used for closing the window shutters and brought a blow down on my shoulder. I sprang off the chair staggering away from her. The hurt was only repulsion at being embroiled with her. I tore the cane out of her hand. Clawing, she came at me with a howl of frustration which seemed to me to reach far beyond our encounter, a howl which came out of the deep of her own troubled life.

I turned her away from me, plunged one hand into her bush of hair, caught my fingers around the belt of her skirt, and propelled her across the room. I threw open the door, and shoved her through, swearing and yelling.

The guard was standing at the end of the corridor, hands on hips in amazement. I latched the door and went out into the garden where I was further away from the frenzy of her cursing and banging on the door, and the shouts of the guard trying to get control of her.

27

The first witness in the morning was Peter Weston. He responded quietly to the oath. His brown eyes were soft and yielding. Under Vale's guidance he confirmed Vaughan's evidence.

Amherst began his cross-examination in a friendly way. "Mr McDade told you his doubts about Trask's guilt?"

"Yes and I arranged for him to see the CO."

"If McDade was right the charge against Trask shouldn't have gone ahead."

"If he was right. The decision was for the CO."

"Did Colonel Vaughan link the charge against Trask with his complaint about the killings on patrol?"

"He said he thought Trask was a troublemaker."

"What did you think?"

"I thought so too."

"McDade is a good officer?"

"As far as I know."

"Don't be mealy-mouthed, Major. He's well regarded isn't he?"

"Correct. I didn't mean to sound ungenerous."

"Can you think of any reason why he would want to lie about Ann James?"

"No, sir."

Amherst ended it there, and it seemed to me that at that point, Vale's case had become a small parochial matter.

Later Vale called Ann James as required by the President.

I was dreading the moment; I could see nothing in her appearance that suggested last night's struggle. She fingered her face with a white hand, wore little make-up and had her hair tied back tightly. She smiled and her presence brought a sense of relaxation to the proceedings if not to me. Vale offered her for cross-examination saying he had no questions.

"She *looks* a clean, decent sort of woman," Amherst whispered. "She ought to go down well."

I was gripped by panic. How wrong he was. Her fury of the previous night dinned in my ears.

Amherst moved toward her radiating friendliness. "You told Colonel Vaughan and Major Weston that Trask was the soldier who assaulted you and another soldier?"

"Yes."

"Tell us what Colonel Vaughan said before you identified Trask."

"He said I'd be held up if I couldn't identify the man. He was determined to find the man and I'd have to wait until the investigation was completed."

"Did that worry you?"

"Yes. We were ready to go. The truck was waiting. I didn't want to miss the next engagement."

"So how were you feeling at the time of identification?"

"I was worried and confused."

"How long was Trask in the room?"

"I don't know. A half a minute. He was behind me."

"You only had a brief glance?"

"I couldn't turn around and stare could I?"

"Had you ever seen him before?"

"I must have. He was one of the crowd."

"And what do you think now about your identification?"

"I'm not really sure who went for me or hit the other guy."

The sweat of fear had oozed from my forehead during her words, but now her vindication of my story exploded in me intoxicatingly.

"You told Mr McDade this before you left camp?" Amherst asked.

"Yes."

Amherst gave the Court a glance which said, "There, you see?" before sitting.

I leaned over to him when she had left the witness stand. "She's lying about Trask. She's fucked him."

Amherst's eyes flickered. "Jesus! How do *you* know?... Never mind, we've finished with her."

When the Court had risen, I said to Amherst, "It looks OK doesn't it?"

"Yes. And it can only be strengthened by your evidence tomorrow."

"Sounds easy," I said without any confidence that it would be easy.

"It won't get you clean away, Bob. The Court is left to interpret your little private ruckus with Vaughan, but it's nickel and dime stuff. A reprimand, maybe."

Vale came over to us, his eyes resting icily on me for a moment. "You've done a good job, Geoffrey. Very neat and economical."

When Vale had moved away, Amherst said, "Tell me how you know Ann James fucked Trask?"

"She told me one reason for identifying Trask was that he hadn't paid her for a screw."

Amherst's good humour had gone. "It's not anything that would hurt your case, but you should have told me. Why didn't you want her called, Bob?"

"Just an emotional 'Ugh!'"

"Nothing factual, huh?"

We parted with Amherst withdrawn. I was escorted back to my quarters. I hurriedly swallowed the dish of noodles that were brought to me. I was restless, excited. I smoked innumerable cigarettes and finished a half-full bottle of whiskey. I went out into the garden in the dark. The air was cool. I stepped onto the grass, my bare feet sinking into the spongey, damp soil. The buildings were dressed lightly in mist. The bushes were black globs, the sky a rich, dark blue. I could hear the distant drone of an aircraft and the thump of thunder – or was it artillery? A few feeble lights glowed, perhaps a cook or a cleaner at work, or a forgotten bulb on an empty stair. Tiredness overcame me like a paralysis. I felt weak and went back to my room to sleep.

A knock on the door awakened me.

"It's half-past nine," Gail said. "You should be up." She stood in the doorway in her captain's uniform looking drained of energy.

I rolled out of bed and gave her an affectionate hug on the way to the bathroom. I shaved, showered and dressed with Gail at the open bathroom door.

"I've got some time off, Bob. I'm coming to the courtroom. I've seen Major Amherst and he seems fairly confident." She saw my stiff grin in the mirror. "You're a little down."

"It's not over yet."

"We'll make a new life for ourselves when we get out of this place, Bob."

"You bet we will!" My surge of affection for her clashed with my memory of what her brother had done. I could see her apprehension in the mirror as I combed my hair. I went on combing long beyond the needs of neatness or vanity.

"Bob?"

The sergeant escort rapped and shouted from the front door, "Ready, Mr McDade?"

"I have faith in you, Bob. Good luck," Gail said, clasping my arm as I passed.

28

Amherst could not help a gleam of assurance when he opened his case.

"McDade's defence is that the argument with his CO did not amount to an assault. McDade was provoked and acted in a self-protective manner. Unfortunately, Colonel Vaughan lost his footing when McDade fended him off. What appears to have ignited the exchange was McDade's reluctance to engage in publicly announcing on parade the punishment of a man whom he believed was innocent."

The Court was attentive and I thought they were influenced by Vaughan's admission that he left his desk and approached me closely. As I took my seat in the witnesses' chair I could feel I had their goodwill. Gail, pale and round-eyed, was at the back of the room. Vale was sunk over his papers, his hand across his brow.

I confirmed the main facts to Amherst. "Did you have any idea where the confrontation was leading?"

"No, I just felt I couldn't participate in the public spectacle."

"What would you have done if Colonel Vaughan had said he would nominate somebody else to deal with the parade?"

"Nothing. In talking to Colonel Vaughan I'd done all I could do. I didn't intend to push him or even touch him. But when he grasped my shirt I pushed him away. I didn't push hard. The fall was caused more by the wet tiles than any force on my part."

Amherst sat down and Vale advanced, blotchy and angry-looking in contrast to the demeanour of the Court. I had a start of fear. He asked many questions, but he was not able to budge me. Then he retired to his papers and seemed confused, riffling them.

"Do you want to go further, Colonel Vale?" the President asked.

"Yes, sir. Mr McDade, how did you know or believe Trask was innocent?"

"I knew him. I talked to him."

"What about Miss James?"

"She withdrew what she'd said to Colonel Vaughan."

"What special connection gave you the advantage of such information?"

Amherst sighed in disapproval. I was trying to appear relaxed, to conceal that my nerves were at snapping point.

"I had no special connection," I said. "I questioned her after she'd spoken to Colonel Vaughan."

"How well did you know her?"

"I'd never seen her before the night of the concert."

"Did you talk to her after the concert?"

Amherst sniffed and shuffled.

"No."

"Any other time?"

"No – wait, casually, and momentarily, before the concert when the hall was being set up."

"You weren't investigating then?"

Amherst interrupted. "Why, sir, are we pursuing this line?"

"Are you objecting, Mr Amherst?" the President asked.

"No, sir," Amherst said reluctantly.

"Let's move on, Mr Vale," the President said, unimpressed either by Vale's probing or Amherst's irritation. "We do have a war out there."

"Just one final question, sir. Mr McDade, have you ever spoken to Miss James or discussed her evidence with her after your investigation?"

I took a great mental breath. The tumult and hysteria of her visit last night reeled through my head in a second. "No sir, I never have."

I looked over the heads of the audience to Gail. Vale signalled his cross-examination was over. My ordeal was over. Neither Amherst, nor the Court had further questions.

"You can resume your seat with counsel, Mr McDade," the President said.

I sat down. Vale rose to his feet.

"I ask leave to recall Miss James."

"Is this really necessary, Mr Vale?" the President said, and then assented reluctantly.

I leaned over to Amherst. "I don't understand."

Amherst cupped his hand over his mouth. "Look, when he asked you about talking to James about her evidence it was a routine question about collusion. Now he wants to ask her the same question. A formality. A waste of time. But he's entitled to do it. Dear old Max flogs on until we drop."

I felt exhausted. My stomach contracted. I pulled at Amherst's sleeve. "Listen, I did see Ann James after the concert and after the investigation. She came to my quarters here."

Amherst's face at first showed astonishment, and then flooded with blood. "You fool!" he hissed. "You goddamned fucking fool!"

He reacted instantly. He stood up. "I ask for a short adjournment, if the Court pleases. The accused is unwell. He's feeling the heat." Amherst handed me a glass of water. "Drink it!" he said through tight lips.

I swallowed the warm, chlorine-tasting water. The President agreed fifteen minutes and the Court filed out of the room. Vale approached looking searchingly at me but exuding a casual air. "You must be feeling confident, Geoffrey," he said to Amherst.

Amherst mumbled a reply and pushed me away to the privacy of a corner near the bench. "So, you've been monkeying with the girl?" His colour remained high red. His voice trembled.

"No, I spoke to her."

"Spoke to her?" Amherst said, contemptuously.

"I threw her out of my quarters last night. I never told her what to say and what she said in court was true."

"That doesn't matter a flying fuck. You told lies on oath, you asshole! Unless the girl tells the same lies, you're finished. Vaughan's story is the only one which will count."

Then Amherst calmed, moved his big head in acceptance. "If you'd told me *all* about the girl, I'd have made sure the true story got on the record. It can't hurt your case. It might hurt your dignity in front of your fiancée, but it can't hurt the case. I might've decided we could do without her if I'd known. Vale didn't want her. I might have got through without her. I only wanted to be a hundred and ten per cent sure."

"I'm sorry," I whispered.

"You're sorry? It's your career and reputation, not mine. You've thrown the case away. At this moment Vale thinks he's on a sure loser. In a few minutes he's going to get a big birthday present, and win an astonishing victory!"

Gail approached us looking worried. "Is there something I can do? I don't know which of you two boys is the most unwell. You both look ill to me."

"Excuse me, Sister," Amherst said, "but I've got to go over some evidence with Bob. We can't talk now," and brushing past her, he pulled me by the sleeve into the hall. At the far end of the hall, out of earshot, Ann James sat on a hard bench, legs crossed, showing her calves and ankles to perfection.

"Can't we have a word with her?" I said.

Amherst fluttered his eyelids and looked upward. "Tempting, isn't it? Perjury we have. Let's not add interfering with a witness."

29

The Court resumed sleepily with a friendly comment on my health. Ann James minced to the witnesses' chair and Vale began to re-examine her.

"Miss James we've heard evidence from Mr McDade about your relationship with him."

"Objection." Amherst was on his feet.

"Sustained," the President said. "Phrase your questions more carefully, Mr Vale."

Amherst whispered to me, "He's trying to bluff her into thinking you've told everything."

"Miss James, what was your relationship with Mr McDade?"

Ann James' face was pale and blank. "Nothing. Not even friends."

"After that casual meeting before the concert, did you speak to him later that night?"

She hesitated. "Yes... he was drunk. After the show."

"At what time?"

"About two in the morning."

"Two in the morning? That's a little after lights out in a war zone." He looked knowingly at the Court. "What did you speak about?"

"Nothing."

"Really? Nothing at two in the morning? Did you have sex?"

"No. I told you, he was drunk."

"Did you ever speak to Mr McDade after you left Camp Dakota?"

She reddened. "Yes, I was angry at getting a summons because I'm missing out on engagements and I went to see him."

"Where?"

"Here."

Vale's eyes were glowing beside his trunk-like nose. "And you talked about the case?"

"There was nothing else to talk about."

The answer seemed to hang in the air. The members of the Court blinked. I felt sick.

"What did you *do*?" Vale asked, his voice thickened by malicious satisfaction.

Ann James' lips had retreated to a thin line of ferocity. She looked at me and I dropped my head. Vale's voice rang out this time.

"What did you *do*?"

"We had an argument. A violent argument."

Vale returned to his seat with a triumphant nod toward the Court. Amherst, deflated, approached Ann James with a small smile and a soft voice.

"Miss James, the argument was about whether you would come to court, wasn't it? Not about what to say?"

"Yes."

"And Mr McDade told you to tell the truth in court."

"Yes."

"And you have told the truth?"

"Yes."

When Amherst sat down, and the click of Ann James' heels had died, the Court bent their heads together conferring, and decided to retire for five minutes. "They're considering the discrepancy between your evidence and the girl's," he said.

I looked round for Gail but she had gone. When the Court returned they had grave expressions. None of the members even glanced at me.

"You're for it," Amherst whispered.

"Proceed, Mr Amherst."

He called me to the witness stand. "Please explain yourself, Mr McDade," he said, casting me adrift.

"In my evidence I denied the connection with Ann James to protect her; and at no time did I attempt to persuade her to tell other than the truth," I said.

I sounded frail. I felt frail. I realised I should have been telling a much better story. I could have honestly said I was ashamed of my drunkenness on the night before the events.

The Court heard me coldly, almost inattentively, and asked no questions. And Vale disdainfully refused the opportunity to cross-examine. I could feel the downward momentum.

"The evidence is closed," the President said. "Do you want to make a closing statement, Mr Amherst?"

Much subdued, Amherst said, "Whatever is said, this case focuses on a physical contact of a trivial nature which ought not to be the subject of a conviction of a brave and loyal officer."

The words fell awkwardly in the air, perhaps judged irrelevant as they were uttered. The President called on Vale.

Now sure of his supremacy, Vale said, "McDade's counsel has endeavoured to show him as a man of integrity willing to help an innocent soldier, but he lied. McDade perjured himself about his connection with the very witness who was supposed to confirm the purity of his motives! Colonel Vaughan's evidence of assault must stand unaffected."

The Court adjourned with the President's promise to give judgment the following morning. I remained seated, head in hands while the courtroom emptied.

Vale sidled over to Amherst. "My, how the wind has changed, Geoffrey," he said with a laugh.

Amherst nodded philosophically.

"It looks bad, but they might… " I began to Amherst when Vale had gone.

"No way," he interjected, lighting a cigarette and pumping out a volume of smoke which engulfed us. "*They will not accept that you could lie on oath*. Finish. End of case. The reason doesn't matter. Do you get that, Bob?"

I reached for one of Amherst's cigarettes.

"Yesterday," Amherst said, "I'd have bet any money that the worst that would happen to you would be a reprimand. Today I wouldn't put a cent on it."

30

That night about 9pm Amherst visited me with a tight smile and a bottle of brandy.

His rage and disgust with me after the hearing had gone. When I said I felt I'd let him down, he said, "It's about being confronted by the totally unexpected. Lawyers don't like that. It's their job to know the facts. They can work with facts they know. They get upset when they find something unexpected. I wanted to win, Bob. I thought we had, as near as hell, won. So I was pissed off with you momentarily. But I like you. And I'm well used to all sorts of human weaknesses. We're not perfect." He held out his hands, palms up, in a rueful gesture tinged with humour.

When we had settled ourselves with full glasses he said, "Now I'm giving you two options, and you have to choose. One, is to take your punishment."

I was surprised to be offered any options. Since Vale had destroyed my credibility that afternoon, I had been virtually semi-conscious. I could see and hear what was immediately around me but I was otherwise numb. "You better tell me what the punishment will be."

"I obviously can't give you a definitive answer, but my guess is reduction to the ranks and possibly a period of detention. Maybe a dishonourable discharge. It's quite difficult for the Court. It's about military discipline and perjury. They know the word will get back to the Regiment."

"Jesus!"

"It *was* trivia; now it's a serious assault. And you're a perjurer, so your explanations will get little credit. Could they possibly take a liberal line about the assault and empathise with a fellow man's sexual delinquencies? Yes, they could, but I wouldn't count on it."

"I don't want to split hairs, but there weren't any sexual delinquencies."

"Bob, I told you, it's all how it looks on the day. With a hard-skinned forces entertainer at 2am in the morning? You could be a virgin. Sure. But try explaining that to the Court."

Amherst seemed to be foreseeing a dangerous voyage to the sentence, with a chance in a million that it might end in calm shallows. "What's the other option?"

"A medical discharge."

I was surprised, despite Gail's comments that suggested I might be ill, and Jim Blake's opinion that I was ill. "How do I qualify for that?"

"By making the most of your headaches and memory failures. The Army psychos will hospitalise you for a while and then discharge you."

"Sounds easy. Why should they do that?"

"Because you'll be talking to them about the massacre at Kam Sung and your friend Blake. Mental illness will weaken or discredit any testimony you might have about that. And you're a perjurer. The Army file will show that. On balance, as far as the Army's concerned, it's better if you're a nut, because you might appeal if you were sane, and confront an appellant Court with Trask's document."

"Could you make anything of that – an appeal I mean?"

"I could make a lot of smoke, implying that you're being silenced, like Trask. But I don't advise it. I doubt that you would win."

"Can you explain why?"

"Why? Because the truth is you're not being silenced, and you'd still have to overcome the perjury taint. Sleep on the options I've given you and let me know in the morning."

I was relieved by Amherst's manner with me and we slouched in our chairs and hypothesised our way through the remainder of the bottle, taking in the lack of progress of the war, and the parts of America that we loved best. We agreed that every day that had passed over recent months failed to clear away the fog which prevented us from sighting the day of victory. While we talked, the options Amherst had given me were lodged in my head like two bricks. When I awoke on the top of my bed at four in the morning, Amherst had gone.

The next morning the members of the Court formed themselves into a sombre line on the bench. I stood facing them.

"We find the accused guilty as charged," the President said. "We consider much of his evidence unworthy of belief, and where there is any conflict with his commanding officer, we prefer Colonel Vaughan's evidence."

Amherst was on his feet immediately. "I have a special application to make. I ask that the accused be remanded for a medical examination and a psychiatrist's report."

The President looked at Vale, who indicated that he was aware of this. "Well, Mr Amherst? A surprise application at this stage."

"My client received a very brief medical before the trial, sir. He did not reveal his serious headaches and amnesia. He has handled matters relating to his defence erratically during the trial, and I believe his judgment is clouded by the trauma of the massacre he witnessed."

"We don't know whether there *was* a massacre," the President said.

"The defendant believes there was, as did his man, Trask, whose report you have seen."

I could imagine the Court considering Trask's complaint. The document contained enough names to credibly justify an investigation, which would be like a poison spring, swelling and seeping to saturate more ground, to suck in more soldiers and pollute their Army.

"At one level," Amherst continued, "this trial has been about a minor and, Mr McDade says, provoked assault by a battle-weary lieutenant on a commanding officer. At another, it has been about the reaction of the same soldier to what he considers is a major war crime."

"Really, gentlemen," Vale said, mild but not too magnanimous in victory. "Could we have a little less rhetoric and a few more facts."

Amherst took his seat and the President invited Vale to respond.

Vale rose and stepped forward with a slight grin as though this wasn't a matter of much consequence. "The defendant presented himself to us as a high-minded officer in a moral dilemma, and he emerged as a venal liar at pains to cover his amatory indiscretions. He displayed a perfectly healthy cunning in presenting his case, and a remand for a medical report should not be considered."

I had the feeling that Vale had not pressed his objection very hard.

The Court adjourned.

I waited in a coma of anxiety with counsel and the military police in the otherwise empty courtroom. Through the open shutters I could see the wilting trees against a searing sky, and the buzzards circling slowly. Vale read a brief for another case and made notes. Amherst smoked and occasionally walked about impatiently in the limited space.

I asked him about my chances. At first, he held his hands up in a denial of certainty, and then became more personal. "They have to be troubled by what might have happened at Kam Sung. It's explosive. I'd give us a ninety per cent chance. Vale agrees. A remand for a psychiatric report tidies up all loose ends."

We waited a long hour. I was remanded for the report.

Amherst and I left the building with my minder, a young corporal from the military police.

I saw the tough grass of the lawn, the worn flagstones on the path, and the sunlight falling vertically through a mist of pollen. Squads of helmeted soldiers marched, light glancing on the white skin of their jaws. A tiny bird flew past the flagpole at the front of the building at speed. The bushes shrugged sensuously in the heat. The sky was green.

"Thanks," I said to Amherst.

"You'll survive. And if, as I believe, you're remanded for treatment following the report, we won't meet again."

We shook hands amicably.

"I'm sorry I've deprived you of a notch in your belt."

Amherst made a throwaway gesture. "I've put you on a plane home with any luck." He half-turned away, and stopped. "By the way, Bob, you might be interested to know that Vale told me this morning that he didn't have any idea of links between you and Ann James. He was flying blind in his questions. He figured he had nothing to lose... These things can turn on a dime."

31

At my billet I dropped my few possessions into a kitbag. I was to return to Camp Dakota in the custody of the MP, collect any necessary kit, and report to the Army Medical Centre at Hoi An. I had 'chosen' the sickness road – assuming the Army doctors believed I was sick – because in common sense there was no other course. And from the moment I'd told Amherst of my decision that morning, I started to wonder and worry if I was sane. I pushed the thought away and re-envisaged myself as I really believed I was: a man determined to manipulate the doctors to my advantage.

The MP was a very tall young man, with his beret tilted forward at a rakish angle and a black and white armband; he sat in the back of the Jeep. I sat next to the driver and braced my legs under the dashboard as the vehicle accelerated away from the wire barricades around the military enclosure, down the road to skirt the town. I had a last look back at the quiet suburb of majestic houses and civic buildings where my fate, so far, had been decided.

The Jeep slewed and canted over as we narrowly missed a cart; we pounded through cobbled streets, missing ditches, stray animals and people by inches. The driver dabbed his horn liberally; he shouted at heedless bicycle riders, and the bearers of bundles of wood who occasionally forced his pace to a crawl.

The flight by Chinook to Da Nang was a routine Army cattle-truck operation; we travelled with a disparate bunch of military and advisers and boxes of supplies in a reverberating hold.

At Camp Dakota, Hoi An, the 33rd Regiment was making ready for action. Trucks were drawn up in lines to await passengers. Full kitbags were piled in front of the huts; machine guns, batteries, wireless sets and ammunition boxes were being stowed. Even in the afternoon heat the men looked jaunty; they would soon be out in lines of defence or on sweep patrols, living in bivouacs and trenches, sharing the strain of constant danger. For a while, some of these huts would be empty – a few days or a few hours – chairs stacked on tables in the mess, the ovens cold, the commander's chair empty and the flagpole bare. Then there would be another regiment, stale and bloodied, showering away the fatigue and the dust and damp of previous days to make a resting place for itself.

I went into the cabin I'd shared with Blake and Boyd and sat on my bunk. The MP remained discreetly outside the door. The mud odour of our clothes, which the laundry could not remove, reminded me of the jungle streams where we had crawled like amphibians. My eye touched a few personal items – a tiny wooden galleon carved by Boyd, Blake's fancy leather toilet case, my own tattered paperbacks – and hung on the walls were all the accoutrements of officers on active service: the belts, gaiters, packs, jackets, capes and caps that I might not wear again. I recalled the pleasure and the pride of wearing these clothes when I first received them.

I packed hastily, leaving the combat gear which would go back to the store, and went outside. The MP had taken shelter in the shadow of the opposite doorway.

"I want to see some people, before we go," I said to him.

The MP nodded, indicating he would not be far behind. I went in search of Blake. I saw some fellow officers in the distance; they seemed to look twice to see if it really was me and then resume their tasks, but they were probably too far away. The news would have travelled. I met Peter Weston on the road and faced his curious, questioning eyes. We talked for a moment about the detail of my departing arrangements, both of us too diffident to refer to the court martial.

When we came to part, Weston said: "You could never have got away with this, Bob. It would have ruined Vaughan and screwed up the Regiment. The Army doesn't work that way. But you've done fairly well by any count."

"Oh, well. A half-win. I'll probably be declared crackers."

I found Blake surrounded by his men. He broke away from them and put an arm round my shoulders quite openly. "You look a little thinner. I heard what happened, Bob. Everybody here knows."

I tried to smile. Blake left his sergeant in charge and we walked a short way down the road, out of earshot, including that of the discreet MP.

"I didn't see how you could get off, Bob, and then I wondered if you wanted to."

"You think I'm trying to get out of the Army?"

"I'll get your kit returned to the store."

"Does Gail know?" I asked.

"Yes, and she understands. You need a rest and treatment and you'll be a hundred percent."

I knew Gail would be pleased at the outcome. I thought she suspected that I was suffering from a trauma. "I'll get in touch with her from the hospital."

Our conversation was awkward and short, partly because the day was too hot to spend talking in the sun, but we finished with handshakes and smiles. I was still unable to determine whether Blake was a friend, an enemy, or a man who didn't care.

I returned along the tarmac in the direction of the barracks, with the MP, and we were overtaken by Sergeant Lucas, streaming sweat.

Lucas saluted. "Wanted to say goodbye, sir. The men send their best wishes. We heard about it – don't understand it. If you have time, sir, to come and see the men... "

My heart expanded uneasily. I had been thinking what to do about the men. I wanted at least to see them, but I suddenly decided against it. "Thanks, Sergeant. I appreciate it. I don't think I can come. I'm... not up to it."

Lucas retired with a shocked look. I asked myself whether my decision showed cowardice, or an understanding that there was nothing to say. What I couldn't explain clearly to myself, I couldn't justify to my men.

32

I was admitted to an assessment ward at Hoi An, and given a small sleeping cubicle. I had to wait a day or two until my file arrived from Saigon and the doctors had had a chance to study it. In the meantime, I received a whole suite of medical tests – blood pressure, heart, kidneys, liver and eyes – and was questioned closely about my headaches and memory. When I was asked about events on the last patrol I genuinely couldn't remember them precisely or clearly, and I gave different doctors different accounts. The immediate past had retreated into a haze in my mind that I couldn't penetrate.

When the physicians had finished with me I was passed to the psychiatrists. They used different techniques. One, Dr Mazengarb, seemed to play the bad guy. He was an ugly man and he had no difficulty in showing rage, contempt and cynicism on his bulbous red face. He sneered at me and questioned my motives. "This is an easy way out, isn't it? Get into civvy street via a nice rest in hospital?" What would an unbalanced man say in response to such prodding?

I said, "What happened, the massacre at Kam Sung, the argument with Vaughan, the court martial, they were things beyond my control. They happened to me." I wasn't going to be unduly defensive about my motives; I didn't need to be; my motives were completely confused.

Dr Mazengarb said, "You lose your case. You come here. Next best thing. If you'd won, you wouldn't be seeking psychiatric help, would you?"

"I don't know. Maybe I would. I seem to have lost the plot."

I began to think that the only way of convincing this guy that I was crazy was to get down on my knees and start barking. But I didn't. I felt too tired and overcome by the examination process. Mazengarb left me with the feeling that he was convinced that I was here on a ruse and had admitted it.

The other group of doctors were the good guys, the friendly ones. They wanted to talk about school and university and Gail and my future. I suppose I gave them a more or less coherent account but even here I had lapses of memory, and so many things I wasn't sure about. It was as though my head had been kicked, and my thoughts, feelings and memories hadn't re-ordered themselves. The doctors particularly wanted to know whether I blamed myself or someone else for what had happened. All I could say was I didn't blame myself or anybody else. I said that as far as I understood it the events all seemed to have their own dynamics and I was merely an onlooker. And now that I was looking back I had to look a very long distance, although Kam Sung was only a couple of months past.

A lot depended on the assessment for me. If I was found to be fit, that is a malingerer, I would be sent back to the Court for sentence.

Gail visited me while I was in the unit. To me she looked fresh and beautiful, although I could see the war's mark on her, a more controlled calm, a more strained smile. She was very affectionate. She seemed pleased that I had been referred for a report and made no comment about the ignominious result of the case. She may not even have known the exact details. The 'story' of what happened no doubt existed in different versions.

"You're in the best hands possible, Bob."

"They may send me back for sentence."

"I don't think so. Nobody can go through your kind of ordeal without suffering trauma."

"That'll mean I'm nuts."

"It'll mean you need a rest, a few months, and some therapy."

I couldn't see the way through to this promised land. The doctors were picking at me, finding every small vulnerability, like vultures pecking at a dry corpse. And the medical onslaught added to a body of dull hurt deep within me. I sought consolation by trying to understand the suffering of some of the other inmates. I couldn't sit down with them and talk; they were creatures in dressing gowns with yellow faces and bandaged bodies who passed me in the hall without seeing, or were wheeled past on gurneys, or lay in their cubicles with the door open, groaning, surrounded by doctors and nurses. They cried out, horrible, hopeless noises. They seemed so much more pitiable than I was, but it came to me after a few hours or days, that I was no different.

"There are some classy specialists in the unit, Bob," Gail said. "You'll be alright. And they're terribly busy. There's no let-up. They've got to make their decisions quickly."

I had detected no hurry or pressure amongst the doctors. They approached me as though they had the whole day to consult. "Maybe there are risks in that hurry for me."

"No, they're humanely cautious. One look at your active service record and the fact that things have gone a bit haywire is enough."

Gail left me, apparently highly confident. Having served for two years I was entitled to be declared crazy!

33

I found my relationship with Dr Meadows, my psychiatrist at the Rochester, New York, Veterans' Hospital, quite congenial. That was presumably what Dr Meadows aimed for. He was a diffident character, but skilled at getting me to talk without being judgmental himself.

In one of our recent sessions, Dr Meadows had told me that I would be fit to be released in a few months. I was taken by surprise. I had become used to the gentle structure of days in the home. I was uncertain what would happen when that framework was removed, or rather I had declined to think what would happen. With Dr Meadows' words, I was once again on the edge of an abyss. It was now more than a year and a half since the Saigon Court had made its finding referring me for a psychiatric report and the Army psychiatrists had diagnosed me as a case of Post-traumatic Stress Disorder.

We were in one of the sun rooms, quiet with thick pastel carpet and deep, soft chintz-covered chairs; it was a gentle and hopeful room. Dr Meadows, not much older than me, was sprawled opposite, tieless, with the sleeves of his pale blue shirt rolled to the forearms. He wore white cotton slacks and soft tan shoes. He had fair hair and a nondescript boyish face, which made me think I might be talking to any young man I met in the supermarket. I suppose I was expecting my psychiatrist to have gravitas.

I realised that these meetings were carefully staged, and I

had come to appreciate them; they were a kind of weekly psychological gym session, and presumably therapeutic.

Dr Meadows had let me talk over the months, often crossing and re-crossing the same ground, usually increasing the depth of my perceptions. He often steered me to find in all that had happened a point of decision, or a point when the die was cast, or a point when the blame for the consequences was clear; a fulcrum for action.

"Why do you do that?" I asked, slightly exasperated on this latest occasion.

"We need to understand what happened, or understand that what happened can't be understood."

"That's the medicine, is it? The serum which will make me well?"

"Yes, if you're unwell."

"How can you cure me if you don't know whether I'm sick?"

"It's the insight you need to move forward, sick or well."

"But *is* there a hinge, something, one particular event or action which caused everything to happen?"

"If there is, we need to find it, Bob."

"But you think we can't, and if we can't, you want me to understand and accept that?"

"Exactly."

"When I went to see Vaughan to try to get Trask's punishment quashed, I was just going to ask him. In hindsight it was a stupid move. The CO had made his decision; he wasn't going to reverse it. I wasn't boiling over with rage. In fact I was apprehensive. Peter Weston tried to persuade me not to do it. I didn't intend the physical contact that happened. I sure as hell didn't see myself as a heroic fighter for human rights. It was just that a man to whom I owed a duty as his superior officer was being blatantly screwed. Events got out of control."

We sat, doctor and patient, watching each other for perhaps half a minute. "Uh-huh. Events out of control," Dr Meadows said. "Any feelings of anger against anybody? Do you want to blame anybody, Bob? Vaughan, Blake, Ann James, Vale, Amherst?"

Dr Meadows had no notes on this occasion; he often surprised me by his mastery of the file, and I had to suppose that behind the boy-next-door look was a penetrating intellect. Eventually, I said, "No. They did what they did, what they could be expected to do, being them. Vaughan was a neurotic, Blake a monster, James a whore. Vale and Amherst, typical lawyers. It was my reactions I guess."

"Your reaction. Do you blame yourself then?"

"I don't feel guilty."

"What do you feel?"

"I accept responsibility. It's my mess. I made it and I should have done better."

"Would you have done better in the trial if you'd handled it in a different way?"

Dr Meadows knew in detail about the trial, but he let me grope around for answers.

"My failure to tell Amherst the truth about my meetings with Ann James? It ruined Amherst's strategy, but it's difficult to admit stupid indiscretions, especially when they have a sexual angle."

"The case was lost because you were unable to admit your drunken adventures?"

"More than drunken adventures. More embarrassment than shame at what I'd done. I *am* engaged to another woman. I care for her. I feared my doings would be noised around the courtroom and outside. It's not easy to say in court, 'Yes I was in bed with this woman, drunk, a venture paid for by a buddy. No, I didn't actually fuck her, I just dozed

163

with my hand on her bare ass for a while.' Not easy to say that. Blake would hear. Gail would hear. I thought we could win without getting into all that shit."

"You thought you could win. What do you think about Amherst's warning to tell him everything?"

"I guess I didn't take it on board. I now see that he couldn't present the best case without knowing the facts."

Another long pause followed. I became aware of the sun beating on me, but a benevolent dry sun, not the torch of Vietnam; and there were yellow begonias in the boxes outside the window.

"Or was it that the events in the jungle had seeped into and undermined your judgment?"

"Maybe. That's where the downhill spiral starts, with me lacerating myself, trying to find the nerve to deal with what happened."

"Or maybe one could put it all down to the fact that you had the bad luck to face a rather relentless and suspicious prosecutor?"

"Sure… any of these," I agreed.

"Or all of them to some degree – and some we haven't mentioned."

"I gather then that you're not interested in analysing the cause, Doctor?"

"I'm very interested, if you can find a cause. I just want you to see that the interpretation of past events can be endless, depending on your point of view. So many reasons, so many motives. Think how Vaughan would see it, or General Mason."

"So there's no point in letting causes bother me?"

"Precisely. It's done. Accept. Move on."

"Not so easy."

Meadows smiled. "But worth working for. The past is only

a fragment in your memory, and a different fragment in the memories of others. We each live in parallel universes."

"I've *almost* put this behind me." In a way, I was trying to show the doctor how responsive I was to his efforts, but the reality was that I hadn't put the jungle or the trial behind me; they continued to torture me and promised to inflict the gravest emotional damage that I could suffer: the loss of Gail.

"Good. Then I almost have a cure."

Another silence. The doctor used silence as a medical instrument. I felt the pressure of these silences, and often started my explanations hurriedly, before I'd thought them through.

"When I'm with Blake I'm also with the Vietnamese woman and the children."

"I understand. So?"

"I don't want to see him. I don't want to be a friend of his or a relation."

The doctor agreed reluctantly. "It makes sense."

"I don't know whether he's a murdering maniac or a hero. You've met him. He looks like a model soldier, doesn't he?"

"He seems a fine man to me. Doesn't his explanation deserve any weight at all – that he was interrogating suspects?"

"Gang rape? Killing children? I was there, Doctor, and with the most liberal view possible, only a little of what happened could be down to legitimate interrogation."

"And yet you didn't intervene."

"I should have, but you don't understand what a dominating presence Jim Blake has."

The sun slanting in the windows had raised the temperature, and faded the light colours of the room. Our shirts showed patches of damp.

"I can't understand how a gifted person like Blake could do what he did," I said.

"He's not necessarily a twisted man, merely a different one. He sees it differently. He wasn't the one who came upon an atrocity committed by another. You think you were. He came upon a bunch of VC or sympathisers who had information that could save lives on his side."

"Children?"

"Children are sometimes soldiers."

"That's a cold, pragmatic way to explain their presence."

"Not necessarily. The heat of battle makes it a real possibility."

"Rape?"

"War is rape. Hasn't every soldier who has had experience of actual hand-to-hand fighting got memories of cruel and inhuman events he'd never have countenanced as a peaceful citizen?"

"Possibly. So standards of behaviour change with the context, but that doesn't justify rape or murder."

"I'm not suggesting that; only that your take on what happened isn't exclusively right, if there is a right one. The experience of life is that we make misjudgements and have misunderstandings, particularly in moments of stress. Often, we don't have the time or space to make corrections. You don't need to hold what happened at Kam Sung against yourself. You effectively made a decision not to intervene. That may have been the right one. What would have happened if you had? It was, from what you tell me, a potentially explosive situation as far as Captain Blake was concerned. You would be challenging his authority. A dangerous thing to do in a dangerous place."

"So I ought to let the past remain inconclusive and move on in the present?"

"Yes. It will help you with Gail. You know life is unpredictable,

Bob; that's why it's both terrifying and wonderful. Everything is chaning all the time."

"But the fact of what Jim Blake did is not inconclusive. And the fact that he's Gail's brother and confidant isn't inconclusive. These facts can't be left behind; they are here now, in the present. And it places a barrier between Gail and myself; invisible, but I feel impenetrable."

"Why?"

"These links mean that I can't have her as my partner without welcoming him."

"Seeing Gail is as painful as seeing Jim?"

"No. She's innocent and ignorant of what happened. But if I love her and marry her I have to embrace her brother."

Dr Meadows scanned the lawns and gardens outside. Servicemen passed the windows: the bent, the lame with their walking frames, the wheelchair borne. What we could see of men, looking out, was pathetic enough, but what was worse was what was going on inside their heads.

"Is there room for forgiveness, Bob?"

"I forgive Jim for myself. I understand that he's a warrior. I never had the guts to complain to him. I understand the pressures on him. But I don't want him in my life. It's the woman and the children that I can't forget."

The doctor frowned at the brightness. "You may be right. Forgiveness won't do it."

"What's the answer, Doctor?"

The doctor's expectant grin which had started the session had been replaced by the emotionless expression of the scientist. "Don't misunderstand me. We're talking now about the present. Your reaction to Gail and her brother *today*. If you believe there's a barrier, there is a barrier, buttressed by a view of past events which may never change." Dr Meadows looked at me steadily. "It's a great pity."

167

34

I was still in the breakfast room at the home at ten-thirty on a Sunday morning yarning with some of my fellow patients when one of the sisters told me I had guests: Colonel Blake and Captain Blake.

I was wearing tan slacks and a figured shirt which Gail had bought for me. I usually dressed on Sundays in smart clothes, ready for any visitors who might come. Occasionally officers from the Regiment or some I'd known in Saigon visited, as well as old college friends and family. It was awkward receiving guests in the home with its polished floors and well-peopled lounge areas; rather like trying to entertain people in a hotel lobby. I was often anxious for them to leave, to relieve the pressure on me, so that I could go upstairs and play cards or chess with my buddies.

Some of my visitors knew precisely how I got here, and they didn't seem to hold anything against me – like weaseling out of the front line, or lying to a court martial. I hoped that any reservations they may have had were subsumed by the label of 'damaged veteran'. With those friends who didn't know precisely what had happened, I was less than forthright, and people are always too diffident to enquire deeply of somebody who has a mental problem.

By and large I could think that Amherst, by getting me referred for psychiatric examination, had saved me from being pitched into the street as a disgraced officer; that was a fate which made me shrivel inside. But there were also times when I wondered what that experience would be like. I would have had to work on my life to restore my own confidence; it wouldn't be a clean fight with observable issues. There would be a cloud of rumour around me scarcely concealing prejudice. I would feel that I had been disloyal to my country and my fellow soldiers. Instinctively, I would want to hide from those who knew me. As it was, I was trying to cope with medical convolutions, and although that was sometimes like jousting with mist, it was an infinitely better state than disgrace. I was, publicly at least, a sick man rather than a discarded failure.

Jim Blake, now a lieutenant colonel, and Gail, a captain, made a patriotic couple in their beribboned walking-out uniforms. Jim had moved steadfastly and quickly upward in the military hierarchy. Gail had kept her promise to leave Vietnam but was anxious to stay in the nursing service until the war was over. She had, however, changed her own focus. She was working with physically and mentally damaged veterans in a hospital near Buffalo. As a result, she knew a great deal more about the medical implications of my condition than I did. I found I was in a dialogue with her which at times, as with Dr Meadows, became a quiet, unacknowledged duel.

I claimed a place for Gail and Jim in one of the small meeting alcoves which were filled with easy chairs and coffee tables; it had bow windows overlooking the brilliant display in the rose gardens: rich velvet blooms of scarlet, orange and yellow. The place and the scene made war almost unthinkable.

Blake had visited once before, a few months ago, entirely himself, brotherly and solicitous as though I was already a member of the family. He never mentioned the killings at Kam Sung, and now that I recollected, never had; I was always the one to allude to them first in the rare conversations we had at the time; and even then, despite my obvious consternation, he never showed the slightest concern about them. He had been through a number of heavy firefights after that incident as he progressed from company to regimental command. Perhaps the most recent horror blotted out the one before. On this occasion we talked mainly about personalities while Gail listened.

Colonel Vaughan had been moved to a staff job after Kam Sung and then resigned. "An emotional man," Blake said dismissively. "Never sound." Jack Boyd was serving in Hawaii. "Still running all his sleazy sidelines." Peter Weston had been discharged sick with an ulcerated stomach. Two of the lieutenants who had joined the Regiment with me had died in action.

I asked Blake about his new command, and he modestly said he was looking forward to getting back to the front line with his men.

Blake asked me when I was likely to be discharged, saying that I seemed very fit and well. I had deliberately avoided telling Gail the latest relatively good news from Dr Meadows because of the problems it would raise. What was I going to do when I left the home, and what part would Gail have in the plan? I had no precise answer to these questions and pushed them out of my mind whenever I thought of them. I liked the veterans' home and I felt safe here. Now Blake, who would expect a straight answer, was pressing me. He wasn't a man you could fob off with bland evasions. He would press until he got a clear view.

I had to say, "I could get out in the next few months", because that was what Dr Meadows had told me. Gail could talk to Dr Meadows at any time she liked about my rehabilitation. He appeared to respect her as akin to a fellow practitioner. Patient confidentiality apparently didn't count.

My intellect was on the dissection table. I knew this from Gail's comments to me about what had passed between me and Dr Meadows. She could find out the truth, so there was no point in saying I didn't know when I might be discharged.

Blake's next question was the one I had predicted about the future. I replied that I would travel for a while, take it easy. I tried to sound a little dazed, tried to suggest I wasn't quite competent to plan for the future yet. Blake said that it was right to come back to civilian life slowly, but was immediately conscious that Gail wasn't mentioned. He glanced at her. She smiled painfully.

"When are you two going to tie the knot a bit tighter than it is at the moment?" he asked.

It was an indelicate question because Blake, despite his cleverness, was brash in human affairs, hardened, brutalised even, by the military life. I couldn't think of anything to say in answer.

Gail filled the gap. She gave a low, humourless laugh and said we were thinking about it.

In recent months, I had gone out with Gail whenever she could get leave and come to Rochester from her posting in Buffalo. She was a good organiser and we always had a planned activity: a walk in the country, a show at a gallery, a movie. We had drinks and dinner afterwards at a quality restaurant. We would hire a hotel room and make love, or sometimes make love in our rental car. I had immersed myself in the pleasure of these carefree meetings. Gail made no demands on me or exerted any overt pressure, but I was conscious that I was being drawn more and more deeply into commitment to her. I was powerless to stop myself. I loved her.

After Gail's remark the air around us seemed to lose its brightness. Twenty minutes of desultory conversation followed and then Blake stood up and took his leave. Gail settled in the chair near me. We watched the slim figure of the young lieutenant colonel as he moved out through the doorway and into the gardens.

"He's a wonderful soldier, Bob. Never a word of complaint about the war, or even anger about the protesters," Gail said.

"Jim just gets on with job. He'll make General for sure."

We sat for a while enjoying the roses; I talked about my visitors and my sessions with Meadows.

Gail leaned over and touched my cheek. "It isn't going to work, is it, us?"

For a long time Gail had been challenged by my withdrawal. But as a nurse she was sympathetic to a wound which would heal in time. As a lover she was perhaps spurred on by love that was not requited as passionately as she wished. She would have been wrong in thinking that I didn't love her wholeheartedly, but I was a divided man. I had bathed in the sensual delights of our meetings without wanting to project our relationship any further. She saw this and suspected my feelings.

I had to face the reality some time soon, and I said, "I don't think it can."

After a silence and a big swallow, she said, "I can't understand why, Bob. We have so much going for us. We have wonderful times together. You would be working in school and I would be at a local hospital. We could have a house in a quiet place, maybe kids, eventually."

I looked at her more closely: the wide, smooth brow, the frame of auburn hair, which just now flamed in the sunlight, the purpled tint of her eyes and the faint freckles on her creamy skin. She shone with sincerity and devotion, and she had just drawn a picture of the life that I wanted with her;

but that life was behind a glass screen and I couldn't go there.

"I guess I'm not all that well." I was hiding behind my illness like the coward I was at Kam Sung, but what else could I do? Apart from telling her the cruel lie that I didn't love her there was no other reason, apart from the unmentionable action of her brother.

"Plenty of soldiers get disordered by their experience and recover. You can't expect it to happen in months. I'm willing to wait." Gail had reverted to the safety of being my nurse and, of course, I had encouraged her by blaming my illness.

"No, you mustn't wait, Gail. I don't know when I'll… "

She reached for my hand and closed her eyes in the sunny, peaceful room. "The disaster of war brought us together and now it seems to be prising us apart."

35

Geoffrey Amherst, my defence attorney, was a surprise visitor on a fine Sunday afternoon a few weeks later. I was just back from the gym and I'd had time to shower and change my clothes. I was feeling very relaxed and looking forward to a walk in town. I didn't want to dig over old ground, but I welcomed him in the downstairs reception room. He was in uniform with an overcoat over his arm and a bulging briefcase; he was nervous and gentle, as he had been at our first meeting. He pulled a bottle of whiskey out of his case but we had to agree we couldn't sit down then and drink. I took the bottle.

"I was in New York and I thought I'd come upstate to see my sister. And I wasn't going to miss seeing you."

Amherst had changed a little since I last saw him, or I was looking at his appearance with more care. He was a little fatter, slightly more bald and his features seemed coarser, but the big head, with its bloodshot slate eyes, was as alert as ever. We walked in the grounds. It was midsummer; the air was light; the sunlight on the flowerbeds a caress.

"Your friend Blake is a half-colonel now with a regiment of his own, Bob."

"I know. He's been in a couple of times. He's having a charmed career."

"He doesn't have any uneasiness with you about killing the villagers?" Amherst looked at me keenly.

"Not at all. He thinks he's right, and I imagine he believes that I accept that. Was there ever an official inquiry?"

"No. I think I'd have heard if there was. The Army buried the investigatory process like Blake buried the bodies, as I anticipated. I'm sure that, for the record, there's a file at 33rd Regiment HQ showing that there was an inquiry at that level, and no evidence was found. Shelving Trask's complaint is thus justified. Does it bother you?"

"I have to live with the memory, and with my part in it, even if, as Dr Meadows says, I shouldn't let it worry me here and now."

"The memory, yes… but you didn't cause it."

"I should have tried to stop it, but I didn't. The truth is I pretended not to notice. I averted my eyes. And even if I couldn't stop it, I should have reported it to my commanding officer and not had a knuckle-head like Trask telling me what my duty was. It isn't a matter of looking back and realising; I knew at the time what I should have done."

"Would it have been out of the question for you to have made your views known to Blake immediately when you met him at Kam Sung?"

"For me it probably was out of the question because I was in awe of Blake, a decorated hero, *and* he was a friend of mine *and* the brother of my fiancée. What would I say? 'Excuse me, Captain Blake (or maybe, 'Jim'). I've just arrived and had a look round and I think you've murdered a few people'?"

"You wouldn't put it like that. You have the words and the craft. Moral cowardice?" Amherst shot one of his sidelong glances at me.

I hesitated, but… "Yes."

"Well, you have to carry the can."

"Yes, as Stefan Zweig wrote, no guilt is forgotten while the conscience remembers."

"You've been over this with your doctor?"

"Every detail, a hundred times."

"That's good. It helps. So what are you going to do when you get out?"

"That's the question that makes my head spin. Everybody asks me. I'm going to keep trying to learn from what happened. Move around the country. Apart from my parents, who are getting on a bit now, and a kid brother, I have no ties. I have a sense that I've been in a cage – much as I like this home – and I'm beginning to think more of roaming free."

"Just hanging out, huh? It has its charms. On the contrary, I'll be putting my experience into the grind of a city practice – New York – when I'm discharged."

"We're on two different roads, Geoffrey. What's happened to the guy who only wanted a small-town practice in the Midwest? That's what you told me. The easy life. Plenty of golf."

Amherst raised his forearms modestly. "I've got the experience, and a connection in New York. Why waste it?"

I could see that the war wasn't *only* killing and maiming, it was capable of changing the values of those who were lucky enough to stay whole and healthy. "Come on 'Victory Day'! If you're as slick as you were in my case, you're going to do very well."

"Maybe you should look at this another way, Bob. If you'd won your case you'd have gone back on patrol and probably ended up full of holes, face down in a stream."

"As it is, I'm a free man with a memory," I said.

Amherst wasn't going to pronounce me guilty of cowardice and after a thoughtful pause he asked me, "How has the treatment been?"

"At first I viewed it as a painful joke; a well man pretending

176

to be ill to escape a worse punishment: shame and disgrace. When I realised I *was* ill and I needed the time here to get straight, I began to feel better."

Amherst looked at me cautiously. "Do you want to hear about Trask?"

Trask had been a constant disciplinary problem for me in the platoon, but more than that he'd been my conscience, gnawing at me during the days after Kam Sung and waking me in the haze before dawn with his knuckles in my spine. "Sure," I said.

"He died in the detention barracks. So apart from you, there's nobody to complain about what happened to the villagers."

"The big machine rolled over Trask, eh? Formidable. How could I have even thought of opposing?"

"Maybe it wasn't that. Perhaps it's mere coincidence. I tracked the item down. He died of heart failure during a keep-fit session."

"He was the kind of guy who would make it harder for himself anyway, a sort of self-induced harrassment."

"Who knows?" Amherst showed the wry amusement of a man who had learned to live with life's chances and conspiracies without being too worried to distinguish one from the other. "In war, the Army, any army," he said, "has a problem about how to deal with the hinterland of violence of its soldiers against civilians."

"It's all there in civil and military law. I don't have to tell you that as a lawyer."

"Yeah. The writing is fine. The problem is that these actions fall into a grey area between legal and illegal. Was Kam Sung a legitimate interrogation or not? In the background there's always the possibility that the Army's reputation will be sullied. No army would wish that on itself."

"I guess that's where I was, and Jim Blake was: in the grey area."

"Right. And Gail Blake, what happened to her?" Amherst's enquiry was polite, almost incurious.

I wondered if I could speak to him, to anybody except Dr Meadows, about my feelings for Gail; but Amherst wasn't merely an inquisitive bystander; he had been the stage manager of a crucial part of my life.

"I care for her enough to understand that I'm not steely enough to shut out what happened at Kam Sung. If I can't do that, I can't see how we can have a life together. Without Kam Sung, we would have married and I believe had a real marriage like my parents'. It's what I wanted and want now more than anything else."

Amherst thought about this, frowned, drew deeply on his cigarette, looking from the placid gardens into the distance, over the lawns to the laurel hedge which bordered the road. The coloured cabs of cars could be seen moving along just over the top of the hedge. Kam Sung seemed impossibly remote. I thought that he didn't really understand and was wondering how ill I was.

"You still see her?"

"Yes, but if you ask Gail, she would say I'm a battle neurosis case who hasn't quite recovered. And in simple terms, I suppose that's true. But I couldn't begin to tell her what I know; it would be like poisoning her mind against Jim, whom she idolises. I couldn't drag him off his pedestal like that either. I don't have the guts. He's a hero to her and to the Army. To me, he's a strange man whom I almost fear, and I don't understand. So there is this blockage in my relations with Gail as palpable as a wall between us. I feel it, and she senses it, but she can never know the reasons... so we have drifted apart, not practically but emotionally."

Amherst considered and said, tentatively, "Are you making too much of this?"

"Every time I see or think of Jim Blake I see that poor abused woman with her legs twisted under her, and the children... How could I marry Gail, join Jim's family, probably see him regularly at family gatherings, and as guest in my house, and a confidant of my wife's for the rest of my life; maybe live a few blocks away, have our children grow up together? On the other hand, how could I tell her? It would be like detonating a grenade over the relationship between three people. Who would she believe? The soldier-hero, or the broken-down veteran? Telling her would be explosive. Not telling her would leave a barricade between us."

Amherst didn't seem to be convinced. "Are you sure you can't talk to her? I mean, the two of you are planning to share the rest of your lives. That's a bigger deal than her relationship with her brother. Some brothers are bad. Some are bad and still loved. Couldn't she swallow that? All you'd be saying is, 'I don't want to be too close to your brother in our life together.' You'd tell her why."

"That sounds very rational. Can you imagine the mental mayhem that she would suffer in the telling? I think you can. But can you foretell what her reaction would be? I don't think so. No way. The chances are that much as she cares for me, she would decide my view of Kam Sung is suspect, unbalanced. Why not believe the strongly and calmly held view of her heroic, unsullied brother? It was an interrogation in difficult and dangerous circumstances. The idea that, after a talk, Gail and I would walk into the sunset together, hand in hand, is impossible to believe. Deep fissures would appear in our relationship. Whether we could negotiate our way over or around these is impossible to say. Let's say we could. It would have a cost in anguish for us both. Is there any point in starting the most important personal relationship in our lives when I know it's going to be riven by this flaw?"

Amherst looked into the distance again, his forehead creased. "Yeah, perhaps you're right that the outcome of a talk could be uncertain… and leave lasting scars. Getting the facts on the table might hinder as much as it helps."

"Because there aren't any absolute facts," I said, "only different views of past events, as Dr Meadows is fond of saying. Talk would be ruinous to the three of us and silence is impossible for me. I can't see any way out but parting, but you don't really agree."

Amherst looked at me out of the corners of his eyes, perhaps wondering if he should oppose. "No, to be frank, I don't agree. I think it's better to face the ugly facts and see what happens. It would hurt Gail, and of course you, but it might lead to a resolution. This is better than turning somersaults, waffling around with 'what-ifs' to protect Gail, with the rest of your life in question. You're proposing to run away from something you should confront."

I merely nodded. We had stated our positions, and we returned to the terrace and had a cup of coffee without returning to the subject again. When Amherst had finished he stood up and we embraced. "I'm very grateful for what you did for me, Geoffrey."

"I guess you won't be around in this area when I'm here next time, but we'll keep in touch," Amherst said.

As he walked away towards the gate, I realised that we had no practical way of keeping in touch. Amherst looked back when he was on the drive approaching the gates. I felt very alone. I knew that at that distance he couldn't see my hollow cheeks or opaque eyes, but I had developed an unmilitary slouch which would have been visible.

Amherst paused again when he came to the low box hedges near the gate. I raised one hand – I was still holding the whiskey – and gave him a thumbs-up with the other. He waved, a resigned, final sort of gesture.

36

My worries about leaving the veterans' home, wondering whether I could stand on my feet, did not go away. Gail was trying to persuade me I was cured or nearly cured, quietly willing me towards the door. And although I had virtually told her we weren't going to make a permanent couple, she ignored it, assuming that once I left the home a well or nearly well man, we would come together and marry. And I didn't want to face the final break with her that would have to come when I was free.

Another thing that worried me about leaving was precisely what I would do. It was one thing to bullshit with Amherst about 'hanging out' and another to decide on how I was really going to spend my hours and days. My parents were too old for me to live with; theirs was the distant, quiet life of two creatures who had become encrusted together in their tiny ambit of happiness. A restless man in the house would only worry them. My kid brother was still in college. I had friends, but no close friends. I couldn't imagine starting teacher training immediately; I couldn't face the concentration of it at the moment. A day is a long time. I feared drifting from bar to bar like so many other veterans.

The routine of the home muffled me, the warmth and the comfort and the casual companionship; and the talks with Dr Meadows. All the inmates in our section were apparently well self-controlled. We had been selected, according to Dr Meadows, because our characteristics were purely psychological, mild and believed to be reversible; we didn't present any violent or dangerous potential. We were surprisingly compatible. We seldom talked about active service although we had all experienced the hardships of it as commissioned officers. We made a good life for ourselves in an undemonstrative way. We dined well, played sport, and engaged in constructive activities like current affairs discussions and debates. We had visiting lecturers on art and books, and we had leisure to read and rest. I was swaddled here, a chick looking out of its nest at a disordered world, and putting off flight until tomorrow.

I had gone for a long period, many months after the trial, feeling that I had fortunately avoided the disgrace of the court martial. Spared from any sentence on medical grounds, I knew I would eventually be discharged sick from the Army. I believed then that I was quite well, and at a time of my choosing, or that of Dr Meadows, I would be able to depart the home and take up my life with or without Gail. It all looked, then, like a clever manoeuvre thanks to Amherst, rather than a disreputable evasion of responsibility.

But eventually my talks with Dr Meadows had become less a psychological game with him, in which I pretended to be a mildly confused person, and more a genuine dialogue between a sick patient and his doctor. I suppose you could say that Dr Meadows convinced me, or showed me that I was sick. Not that he ever said so. It simply became apparent from the weight of his questioning that I didn't see things clearly and must be sick.

What Dr Meadows did was to point out to me that I didn't know Jim Blake or Colonel Vaughan or Darrel Trask and they didn't know me. What he meant was that you couldn't *know* another person. You might think you did, especially, say, a sister or a brother, but you could never really tell with certainty what they were thinking or how they were going to react. He said people with the best possible motives were always misunderstanding each other, leading to differences, and often violence. Each person was unique and had a unique take on events – that was why human relations were so interesting and at times, so bad.

This was why he concluded that in my case it wasn't any use taking a particular position about what happened at Kam Sung. To him, the idea that the massacre could be seen as an incontrovertible fact was simply wrong. Therefore there was no reason to go out on a limb for one particular interpretation or another. He said I could, by all means, have my own view, but I always had to recognise that it mightn't be right. And this recognition of fallibility ought to be a corrective for me if I was inclined to blame Blake or Vaughan or Trask.

Actually, I found this a helpful insight, thinking in terms of my personal guilt, but I began to have nightmares and headaches because I came to understand that I was indeed cast into a world where people didn't know each other, the half-blind leading the half-blind. Dr Meadows was very candid in saying that all the evidence was that people were self-interested and selfish, and that the pursuit of our desires was what drove us. That pursuit was what made us suffer because we could never achieve our desires or completely satisfy our wants. He believed that life was suffering and the only way you could deal with it was to eliminate your desires, to accept the way things were. With this thinking the world both outside and inside my nest appeared to me to be more bleak than I ever thought it was.

The nightmares, which were all different, had a common pattern: an enticement or some imagined urgency to leave a place of safety and enter a place, a town, a house, or a road or rail system where there was superficial order, but underlying disfunction. I had to find my way but I could not. I lost small possessions on the way, like my watch or my wallet or some clothes, and made frantic but failed attempts to find them. Maybe these were exaggerations of what scared me – leaving the home. Sometimes at the conclusion of the nightmares I was cast into that place which terrorised me; it was dark, disjointed, and created a deafening ear-drum piercing noise, the grinding noise of trains, of screaming jets and heavy artillery. I would awake sweating and yelling, with an ache like a piece of hot metal in the centre of my skull.

Dr Meadows wasn't worried about my nightmares and headaches. He seemed to take them as a matter of course. I had a brain scan and there was nothing organically wrong with my head. Was this just a phase of healing? Dr Meadows thought so. I didn't think so. I thought my condition hadn't improved – as Dr Meadows insisted it had – but had worsened. I didn't think Dr Meadows was actually driving me mad; that was a thought too far. But what he had done was to identify a 'reality' – my own personal and unique reality – which was nihilistic and too awful to face.

Yes, he had given me the clue to nirvana – acceptance – but it was a small gem buried in the tumult of my imagined problems. And I knew it was there. I just couldn't deal with it; I couldn't bring it to the forefront of my being.

Therefore, I reasoned that the only way for me to relieve myself was to leave the home; to go out into that crazy 'reality' that unnerved me. The agreeable Dr Meadows, with his many gentle insights, was prolific with drugs, and my nights and days now were often spent on my bed in a languid daze in which my mind was stuck with his conclusions about me.

I could now have left the home on my initiative alone. I had no obligations. My discharge had come through. I had money in the bank. My continued treatment was by consent, unless the doctor felt I was cured, in which case he would discharge me. Feebly, I chose to enlist aid from Gail. Was this a wrong move? When I first told her I wanted leave, she behaved like a nurse and said I had to go when the doctors regarded me as cured. But the lover in her eventually got the upper hand over a period of weeks. And she was certainly influenced by my protestations that I believed I was getting worse, not better.

I don't know for sure, but I'm inclined to think that Gail spoke to Dr Meadows about me, probably revealed what I was thinking. But he was the sanguine, confident type unlikely to be swayed in his judgment or his treatment by a side-wind. He had a shell of professional arrogance, likeable as he was. And he also had a *what the hell, nothing really matters,* attitude to patients. His kind of medicine was hit or miss anyway, so what if this vet or that was retained or discharged wrongly?

Gail collected me in her car one afternoon. I took my best clothes with me and a few books. I left a letter of explanation for Dr Meadows and one for my buddies, and I left all my pills.

37

I moved into Gail's small apartment in Buffalo, near to the hospital where she worked. It was a very cozy apartment and it would have been ideal if it hadn't been so close to the Buffalo State Veterans' Hospital. I wanted to get away from the hospital as an idea and a reality. However, Gail was committed to her work and for a month or so we enjoyed being together, and I said nothing.

I even agreed to go with her to see her workplace. She wrongly assumed I would be impressed. Certainly, it was an impressive place of its kind, and doing astonishing work repairing broken people. I had simply had enough – too much. But I said nothing. I smiled. I joked a little. I allowed her to conduct me through pristine, well-staffed, ultramodern wards equipped with probably every technical device which could in some way relieve the agony of the wretches who lay there in their beds. I silently congratulated the humanity of a government which could assemble this care, while I cursed the inhumanity of a government which caused the need for it. I tried to remember the Bob Dylan lyric about the death of Medgar Evers, where nobody believes they are to blame.

Gail showed me the shining operating theatres and I saw them as shining meat-processing plants. "Remember the unfinished one at Hoi An?" she asked with a laugh. I recalled a moment of ecstasy from a different life.

She explained that teams of surgeons were brought in to

perform the most intricate procedures. They tinkered with hearts and nerves and brains and bones in unimaginable ways. The results lay in the beds and wheelchairs around the building, or in the mortuary.

Gail worked in the neurological department and the wards were chambers of horrors to me. Soldiers once so heroic-looking in their helmets and flak jackets, fighting *and winning* in the mud and dust, were now strapped and bandaged in beds and wheelchairs; they were fitted with grotesque supports and stays and braces for their heads and limbs; some were bandaged with only a little protesting, pink flesh showing, or a rolling, terrorised eyeball. And then there were the men whose limbs appeared to be intact, gowned, sitting on their beds, shoulders slumped, like starving herons by a dry lake, staring with wary eyes at us: the immaculately uniformed captain of the Nursing Corps, and her pale and thin, grey-suited visitor, strolling on the shining rubber floor.

I noticed a difference between the ward where I had stayed until recently and these ones of Gail's. At Saratoga Springs we had been a mild and gentle crew, sedated into a mild and gentle routine; we played cards quietly and discussed politics and the country's economy. Even if we argued it was in a dry, academic way. We were in a cushioned space between the clinical chill of hospital, and the noisy nightmare outside, trying to believe that the nightmare could be faced.

Here in Buffalo, there was a sense of shadows behind a curtain. Outwardly there was order, a strained quietness only broken by the odd moan or cry. What might be behind the curtain in the mind was only betrayed by a soldier's occasional unwavering eyes, or an enigmatic half-smile – the knowledge of the fearsome and mindless void where they were now; a void which I knew was filled with thunderous noise and searing heat.

The horror of war, I had found, wasn't in the blast of bombs, or the whisper of bullets, or the stench of corpses, or the suffocating mud of the jungle, or the lunatic order to attack; the horror was afterwards, when you were shipped home and you had to get up from your bed in the morning and face the screaming anarchy of your broken mind.

I shivered.

When we came out of the ward into the sun on the patio I was in a dark cloud.

"What's the matter, Bob? You look upset."

The sun warmed my face. I saw that the garden, exquisitely colourful as it was, had been planted in rectangles and squares of flowers, shrubs and small lawns. The shrubs, hedges and lawns were so neat that they might have been clipped with a pair of surgical scissors. The architect had created straight lines that joined other straight lines, in a frightening attempt at a kind of rectangular sanity. I knew that actual existence couldn't be like that; it was full of jagged lines and curves which bent and crossed and jarred on each other.

"I can't stand it in there, Gail."

"Of course, it's horrible in one sense, Bob, but in another it's a marvellous place. I thought you'd like to see the difference from the Springs... and maybe see how well you are in comparison."

"Thanks, I do. Or I think I do... It's a kind of prison. It's hell, with air conditioning and clean linen."

"Yes, but we're doing good work. Don't you see that, Bob?"

"Sure, but do *you* have to do it? You've already done more than plenty. I mean, I know how you felt in 'Nam."

"I chickened out. I couldn't take it. Not that close. I was a little ashamed of myself, but it was self-preservation."

"I thought you might like to get out of the Army."

"Not until it's over, Bob. I quit once, but I know I can handle this, what I have here."

"But the mangled and mutilated vets won't stop coming until long after the day of victory, whenever that is; and there'll be more, hundreds more with every month that passes *before* then."

"I can handle it. I must. The day of victory as you call it is the date I've set myself."

"You've done enough, Gail."

"Not until that day. I owe it to Jim and to those guys in there," she said, pointing to the door.

"You sound like Jim. You owe him nothing that you can deliver by service here."

"He's my brother and I love him and he's putting his life right on the line. You'd expect me to sound like him, wouldn't you? Don't you want me to go on with nursing?"

"Nursing, yes, Gail, but not nursing vets. I'd like to get away from everything connected with being a damaged vet: hospitals, psychiatrists, crazy guys. I want to get out there where people live ordinary, peaceful lives and do all the boring things. I want to work quietly, probably as a teacher, read the newspapers, watch baseball, mow the lawn and have a couple of kids with my loving wife."

Gail was silent. She was thinking. Her eyes were wet, and her cheeks. But she was otherwise composed. She put her head on my shoulder. "I want those things too. The war has ripped our lives apart. We're both damaged vets."

38

Gail and I remained on terms which were outwardly affectionate. We didn't argue. We enjoyed sex. I used my days walking around the town and on trails in the woods and reading, hardly thinking, trying not to think. In the evenings I sometimes cooked for Gail or she for me, and we went to the cinema and football games. At times we met friends of hers at restaurants or bars.

But a big unresolved space had opened up between us. We both understood this and stepped back. She understood with clarity the aversion I had developed for veterans' homes from the moment I mentioned it to her on our visit to her department. I didn't have to repeat or explain it. She might even have thought that my reaction was normal enough. At the same time, her commitment to continue to nurse damaged vets was inspiring and of vital importance to her; it was more than just an idea or a plan. I couldn't mistake her sincere resolve from her words at the hospital.

My problem with Jim Blake also remained unresolved; it was always flickering at the back of my consciousness when I was walking and trying not to think. But I *had* thought, and I had just about decided to adopt Amherst's advice and tell Gail. It was an approach which was honest, if cruel for her, but I had come to believe it could be worked through. I had to face my version of reality; Gail too had to understand it.

I knew that Gail would never ever believe that her

brother had committed a war crime. She would regard my version of what happened at Kam Sung as the delusion of a sick man. And why shouldn't I let her take that view? At the same time, I would be saying, "This is my view and my feeling. I may be wrong." I would be arguing that the two positions were not mutually exclusive. Meadows' argument was that what happened in the past depended on the viewer. We could adjust our lives with the ulcer of Kam Sung in mind; in practice, she could keep me sufficiently clear of Jim and his life for it not to become inflamed. I loved Gail; I was prepared to compromise and I thought Gail too was strong enough to compromise. And my own feelings about Jim Blake would probably weaken over time; they were in the nature of revulsion; there was nothing aggressive towards him in them.

The new problem I had to cope with was Gail's work and the constant shadow of damaged vets in both our lives. The spectre of becoming a damaged vet had haunted me – and probably all those on frontline service – during my entire time in the Army. And that spectral fear had been expanded and sharpened from the time I met Gail. Her work and the *need* to talk about it made the threat of damage more real and seemed to bring it closer. Having sex in an operating theatre! Gail suffered the same fear by proxy, for me, for her brother and for her charges; it had driven her out of 'Nam.

Surely, Gail's determination to continue her work with vets – laudible and, for a woman like her, perfectly understandable – was capable of compromise too? It was 1970, the day of victory would come soon, or we could agree a time limit on her service. Two years? I could handle that. I'd be up to my ears in teacher training or sorting out a new career. All I wanted was the understanding that after a reasonable time we would banish this present scene.

I decided I would speak to her at a moment when we had the leisure to reason, maybe in bed on Sunday morning. I was cheered by this resolution. I could see a path ahead, a difficult but ultimately worthwhile path.

Gail was a senior supervisor and rarely worked at night except to cover a staff shortage. However, on one such night I was in the apartment alone preparing my dinner. I had completed a brisk five-mile walk in the afternoon and had a shower. I planned to read in the evening until Gail came home about 11pm – the *New York Times*, and then something serious: Conrad's *Heart of Darkness* and Achebe's *Things Fall Apart* (if you feared you might be mad I thought it might help to examine our collective madness). I was going to dine on cold cooked salmon and salad, with a sweetcorn cob to start. I had set the table and put the cob on the gas to boil. For company while I worked, I had switched on the local television news. I wasn't watching or listening, at least not with any real attention; the screen was above the sideboard behind me.

I became aware that the screen voices were suddenly excited, almost frantic. I turned around to see the red tag on the screen: *Breaking news*.

For a moment, all I could discern was a jumble of lights flaring in the darkness and the howl of sirens; not one siren, but several; then the white bodies of police cruisers. The camera jumped from scene to scene. A five-storey building lit by garden lights. A road packed with white cruisers. A knot of police and officials on the kerb talking with tense gestures. The dark figures of people running between the building and the roadside. The gradual formation of a cordon of police officers in front of the building. The clatter of a helicopter above. Searchlights fingering the houses and trees. An aerial view of the building with illuminated gardens.

And then the voice over: ... *This tragic scene... the Veterans' Hospital in Richmond... the police and emergency services were called an hour ago... too late to avoid the tragedy of a man believed to be armed with an automatic rifle who entered the building and fired indiscriminately at patients and staff... we understand the man proceeded through the wards, firing... He finally barricaded himself on the roof... Military Security Police have pinned him down and are attempting to persuade him to give himself up...*

The sickening fact thudded into my consciousness. This was happening in real life a block away, and Gail was on duty in that building! I turned off the gas, changed into street clothes and ran the block to the hospital. I was there in minutes. I came to a police tape and a cop waved me away.

"My fiancée is in there!"

"Sorry buddy. Keep away. Give the services space."

"How can I?"

"You can't go in there."

Other people were beginning to gather on the sidewalk and road, some of them possibly with loved ones inside, but mostly just curious.

"Do you know what's happening in there? Does anybody here?" I asked, loudly.

"The military are taking care of it," a cop's voice said.

Another cop chimed in, "They'll blow the guy's ass off."

I thought there *must* be a supervisor who could explain more, and I moved along the cordon. Bodies were being stretchered out to ambulances. I approached one of the medics.

"Do you have a log of who these people are?"

"No, sir. This is an emergency. We gotta get them to accident and emergency in town, St Martin's, quick-smart."

"My fiancée is in there."

"I'm sorry sir, I can't help you."

I pushed past people to the hospital gates. I found a senior cop with gold braid on his uniform. When I could get his attention I said, "My fiancée's in there."

"This is not a police command. The hospital is a military establishment," he said.

I heard a burst of automatic rifle fire from inside the building. "You don't know anything? What in hell are you *doing*?"

His mouth tightened. "We're liaising with the military and providing support, sir."

I wanted to ask him if there was anybody giving information to friends and relatives of those inside, but his attention was claimed by somebody else. I strode through and around the crowd like a demented man, looking for somebody who knew something. The bodies were still being taken to the ambulances. "But *this* is a hospital," I said to a man near me who appeared to be as confused as I was.

"Guess it's a mite fucked up in there," he said.

I collided with another man wearing a press badge and carrying a camera. I clamped his arm. "Can you tell me anything? My fiancée's in there."

"Reckon about twenty-five. Highest I've heard."

"Dead?"

"Yeah."

"Injured?"

"No clues. It's always more, isn't it?"

"Shit. Why isn't anybody in charge out here?"

He began to ease past me. His lip curled. "Army screw-up. One of their own nutballs beat their security."

I looked at my watch. I had been prowling through the crowd for ten or fifteen minutes, but it felt like an hour, getting nowhere. No message from Gail. She would know I would be worried, and one of the first things she would do would be to call me at home.

There was a possibility she had somehow left a message at the apartment. I raced back up the block. She could well be too busy to call, looking after the injured, but…

I burst into the apartment. No message. The television was still on, and on the story. The banner at the foot of the screen said it in few words. *Siege at Veterans' Hospital over – gunman dead.* I watched the dead-pan presenter, a cherubic young blonde. *We learn that there were tense moments when it was believed that the lone shooter would give himself up in response to requests from Military Police… however it's reported that at the last moment he came out from cover threateningly with his weapon ready for firing… Military Police marksmen say they had no alternative but to shoot… The only information we have about the shooter is that he was an inmate of the hospital about to be discharged… We can't give you the total number of people killed in the shooter's earlier attack, except to say that it is believed to exceed fifteen… Identification of those killed and injured is proceeding as we are on air… We will be returning to this story during the evening…*

I took the keys for Gail's car and drove to St Martin's Hospital A&E to see if Gail was amongst the wounded. My frantic enquiries led me to join a group of about five people who were on the same errand; they were as distraught as I was.

I half-listened to an official telling us what the procedure was. "I'll pass round this list of those we have identified," he said. "Two men have not been identified."

The paper moved quickly through the group with cries of anguish as people discovered or failed to discover the person they sought. Some people moved the list in front of their eyes as though their eyes had failed; I think I was the last to see it. Gail's name wasn't on the list. My heart felt as though it was bursting in my chest.

Gail had her name on her uniform, and on a security card around her neck. She would have been easy to identify if she was injured. It was pointless me considering unidentified people, and I had to wait while the official outlined the procedure for this.

"How do we find out the names of those who have died?" I asked when he was through, my voice dry and thin.

"Well, it's for the military. I'm sure they'll make an announcement as soon as possible."

"As soon as possible must be now."

"Yes, quite possibly. At the Veterans' Hospital. We're only concerned here with the… "

I walked out and drove back to Gail's apartment. Inside, the television blared in the darkness; now focusing on a car wreck on the interstate highway. No message from Gail. No message. I called the Veterans' Hospital. A tape reeled over. *If you are enquiring about the tragic shooting at the hospital tonight, please be aware that we cannot release the names of the victims until the next of kin have been notified… and please note that all injured personnel are being treated at St Martin's Hospital… press one for all other business…*

I pressed one. A male operator came on the line. "It's about my fiancée… "

"If it's about the incident here tonight, I'm sorry, sir, but we can't… "

"Suppose I was her next-of-kin, her brother… ?"

"If you were next-of-kin we would call you."

"When?"

"Those calls are going through now."

Nobody would call me. I wasn't kin. I was unknown. I shut off the phone and ran the block to the hospital. The scene was still lit up. The crowd had shrunk. The tapes twisted in the breeze. Two empty cruisers with small red lights glowing inside were at the kerb. A few police stood around silently. At the hospital doors inside the gates I could see military police. Some people were coming out, probably crippled with grief but in the night light it didn't show.

I spoke to the nearest cop: "Can I go in there?"

He squinted at me impassively. "No, sir."

"But my fiancée works in there! She's a nursing supervisor. She's not amongst the injured at the hospital. She hasn't called me… "

He shook his head slowly, negatively, not really listening.

Another group of men stood at the curb by the gate muttering. I had no idea why they were there; they might have been ambulance drivers or press or even lost hearts like me. "Can I go in there?" I said in a loud voice, which broke into their talk. "I want to find out if my fiancée is dead."

The loud almost, hysterical word 'dead' stirred them. The men gave me wrinkled looks; they seemed to have heard so much bad news that they couldn't be involved in any more. "I don't think so… " one of them said, weakly.

My temper was rising at the impotence of those around me, and my own. I was determined to get inside. I passed the cop at the gate without looking at him, and started down the path, walking fast, eyes front. I heard the clatter of steps behind me, and felt tight hands grasping each of my arms. I was dragged backwards to the gate by two cops, my heels scraping along the ground.

"Get this, buddy. You aint goin' in there! Now git out and go home!" one of them shouted.

I went back to the car, agonised by the certainty that if I entered the hospital I would only confirm what I already knew.